# Her Seven-Day Fiancé

—

## Brenda Harlen

**HARLEQUIN®** SPECIAL EDITION

Recycling programs
for this product may
not exist in your area.

ISBN-13: 978-1-335-46579-5

Her Seven-Day Fiancé

Copyright © 2018 by Brenda Harlen

**Printed in U.S.A.**

www.Harlequin.com

## "I have a confession to make."

"What's that?"

"Even before we sat down to eat, I'd decided to give this fake dating thing a shot."

"Why?"

"Because of the kiss," Jason admitted.

"The kiss?" Alyssa echoed.

"Since that brief but potent kiss across the bar at Diggers', I've found myself increasingly preoccupied with the thought of kissing you again."

"You have?"

He nodded. "And it occurred to me that I've been remiss in my boyfriend role if that was our first kiss after three months of dating."

"That's one explanation," she acknowledged. "Another is that we haven't actually been dating for three months."

"That does seem like a more credible reason," he acknowledged. "But if we're going to convince your parents that we've been dating for— Actually, it would be closer to four months by Memorial Day weekend, wouldn't it?"

"I guess it would."

"Then you're going to have to get used to me kissing you."

\* \* \*

**MATCH MADE IN HAVEN:**
**Where gold rush meets gold bands!**

Dear Reader,

Haven is certainly living up to its name for high school science teacher Alyssa Cabrera. The Southern California transplant loves everything about the northern Nevada town: her new job, her new apartment and especially her newfound freedom—if only her mother would stop matchmaking!

Nevada native Jason Channing would be quite the catch, if he had any intention of being caught. But he can't deny that he's hot for the new teacher in town, and when his neighbor asks for a favor, he's just a guy who can't say no—not even when she tells him that what she needs is a pretend boyfriend for a few days.

Somehow a few days turn into a few weeks, until a chance encounter with her family upgrades his status—to fake fiancé!

But there's no cause for panic, because they're only pretending to be in love...aren't they?

I hope you enjoy Alyssa and Jason's story and will look for the next installment in my Match Made in Haven miniseries. *Six Weeks to Catch a Cowboy*, coming September 2018, is the story of rodeo star Spencer Channing who inherits a little girl—and is racing against the buzzer to find a mommy!

All the best,

*Brenda Harlen*

**Brenda Harlen** is a former attorney who once had the privilege of appearing before the Supreme Court of Canada. The practice of law taught her a lot about the world and reinforced her determination to become a writer—because in fiction, she could promise a happy ending! Now she is an award-winning, RITA® Award–nominated national bestselling author of more than thirty titles for Harlequin. You can keep up-to-date with Brenda on Facebook and Twitter or through her website, brendaharlen.com.

### Books by Brenda Harlen

### Harlequin Special Edition

#### *Match Made in Haven*
*The Sheriff's Nine-Month Surprise*

#### *Those Engaging Garretts!*
*The Last Single Garrett*
*Baby Talk & Wedding Bells*
*Building the Perfect Daddy*
*Two Doctors & a Baby*
*The Bachelor Takes a Bride*
*A Forever Kind of Family*
*The Daddy Wish*
*A Wife for One Year*
*The Single Dad's Second Chance*
*A Very Special Delivery*
*His Long-Lost Family*
*From Neighbors...to Newlyweds?*

#### *Montana Mavericks: The Great Family Roundup*
*The Maverick's Midnight Proposal*

#### *Montana Mavericks: The Baby Bonanza*
*The More Mavericks, The Merrier!*

#### *Montana Mavericks: What Happened at the Wedding?*
*Merry Christmas, Baby Maverick!*

Visit the Author Profile page
at Harlequin.com for more titles.

This book is for the teachers
who go above and beyond to make a difference in
the lives of their students, especially Robin Meyer,
Michelle Sandoval and Lori Faccio.
Thank you for all that you do!

## Chapter One

No one would ever describe Jason Channing as a morning person—especially not before he'd had at least his first cup of coffee. And yet, he used to set his alarm for 7:00 a.m. every morning, at which time he'd slap the clock to silence the annoying buzz, drag himself out of bed, pull on a pair of shorts and a T-shirt—or jogging pants and a sweatshirt, depending on the season—lace up his running shoes and head out for his 5K run.

It was a pattern he'd established in high school, when he was a quarterback for the Westmount Mustangs and his coach had insisted that routines and discipline were even more important than talent in building a winning team. Jay hadn't played ball in more than a decade, but he continued to run every morning. And for the past two months, he'd had an extra incentive to hit the pavement: Alyssa Cabrera.

The Southern California transplant had moved into unit 1B of the A-frame triplex sometime near the end of the previous summer. He hadn't paid too much attention to his new neighbor at the time—although he'd done a double take that first day, and that second look had reinforced his first impression of the new resident as a definite knockout. But preoccupation with his fledgling business and his own relationship rules had discouraged him from doing anything more than look.

Until one morning in early March when he'd awakened before his alarm and decided he might as well start his day. He'd headed out for his run at 6:45 a.m., just as Alyssa was returning from hers. She was wearing a hoodie, body-hugging leggings and high-end running shoes that suggested her morning routine was more of a passion than a hobby.

He'd awakened an hour earlier the next morning in an effort to sync his schedule with hers. And though she'd initially seemed wary of his request to join her, she'd consented. So he'd set his alarm for the same time the next day again. And the day after that, because it was a pleasure to spend time with a woman who didn't feel the need to fill the silence with idle chatter. As the days turned into weeks, he found that his daily exercise—even now starting at 6:00 a.m.—had become more of a pleasure than simply a habit.

Aside from those early encounters, their paths didn't cross very often, despite the fact that they lived in the same building. As a math and science teacher at the local high school—that much she'd revealed in between sprints—she worked the usual school hours Monday to Friday, while Adventure Village, the family-friendly activity center he owned, required him to be on-site from early to late Wednesday through Sunday.

Then, completely out of the blue and in the midst of a March blizzard, she'd shown up at his door with a covered dish in her hands. Apparently the unexpected storm that had shut down the town had also canceled a staff potluck at the high school, leaving Alyssa with enough chili to feed twelve. She'd already put a container aside for Helen Powell—the widowed resident of 1A, who was out of town visiting her daughter's family—but she still had more than she could possibly store in her freezer.

As Jason had listened to the explanation of why she was at his door, he found himself mesmerized by the curve of her lips rather than the words she was saying. And when his gaze had dipped lower, he couldn't help but appreciate that her soft sweater and leggings outlined her sweet curves. She wore fuzzy socks on her feet, and the top of her head barely reached his chin, but there was a lot of punch in the petite package.

Since the storm prevented him from going anywhere, he'd invited her to come in to eat with him. He'd opened a bottle of merlot and, as they'd shared dinner and conversation, he'd found himself increasingly intrigued by the beautiful woman he'd never really let himself notice before.

After that night, when they'd sipped wine and listened to the wind rattling the windows, he'd been much more aware of his neighbor—and more cognizant of her comings and goings. But their morning runs had done little to satisfy his growing curiosity about his new neighbor.

"Looks like spring is finally here," he noted, when he met her at the top of the driveway on a Friday morning in early May.

"The last time you said that, we got dumped with six inches of snow only a few hours later," she remarked, walking toward the street.

"No chance of that today," he promised. "The sky is clear and blue."

"So far," she acknowledged.

They turned west, away from the rising sun, and picked up their pace.

"Any big plans for this weekend?" he asked as they transitioned from a brisk walk to a slow jog.

Her only response was a negative shake of the head that sent her ponytail swinging from side to side.

"You're not going to ask if I have plans?"

"I don't need to ask if a man whose nickname is 'Charming' has weekend plans," she noted.

He winced inwardly at her use of the moniker he'd thought—*hoped*—he'd outgrown. "Where'd you hear that name?"

"In the staff room at school."

Of course. Because he'd dated Lisa Dailey, the music teacher, Shannon Hart, the girls' gym teacher and soccer coach, and—very briefly—Taylor Lawson, the office administrator.

"Rumor has it you've broken the hearts of all the single women in Haven and are dating someone in Battle Mountain now."

"Was," he clarified.

"She dumped you already?"

He was so surprised by the question, he stopped running.

It took a few strides before she realized he was no longer beside her and turned back, jogging on the spot until he caught up again.

"She did *not* dump me," he told her.

"You dumped her?"

"We decided that we wanted different things," he said as they continued along their usual route.

"She wanted a relationship and you didn't?" Alyssa guessed.

Her assumption hit a little too close to the truth for comfort. "Renee said that I was too focused on my business and not enough on her."

"And instead of trying to appease her with flowers or chocolates or candlelit dinners, you gave her the equivalent of a relationship pink slip."

"Pink was her favorite color."

She surprised him by laughing. "Then maybe you made the right decision."

"What's your favorite color?"

"How is that relevant to anything?"

"It's a simple question—although also a personal question," he acknowledged. "And I've noticed that you always sidestep personal questions."

"Orange," she told him.

"Why orange?"

"That's an even more personal question."

"Tell me anyway," he urged.

She picked up her pace and turned onto Peregrine Lane, and for a minute, he didn't think she was going to answer.

"Because it's the last color you see as the sun dips below the horizon at the edge of the ocean," she finally responded.

"That's right—you're a California girl, aren't you?"

"Former California girl," she amended.

"Why'd you trade sand and surf for northern Nevada desert?"

She shrugged. "It was time for a change."

"Sounds like there's a story there."

"Did you date Belinda Walsh, too?"

"I don't think so," he said, a little warily.

"She teaches English at the high school," Alyssa explained. "And she looks for hidden meaning in everything."

"That's not a female thing?"

She sent him a disapproving glance. "Belinda was talking to another teacher in the staff room one day, explaining the symbolism in a poem her class was studying. She claimed that the blue curtains fluttering in the breeze were representative of the author's depression. I suggested that perhaps the author just happened to be writing in a room that had blue curtains."

He grinned. "Sometimes a cigar is just a cigar?"

"And sometimes orange is just the color of a sunset," she confirmed, waving to him as she made her way to her door.

Clearly that was all she intended to say about the subject, but as Jay made his way up the stairs to his own apartment, which occupied the two upper floors of the building, he wasn't entirely convinced. In fact, he suspected there was a lot more going on with the sexy schoolteacher than she wanted anyone to know.

He did know that she left her apartment at precisely seven twenty-five every weekday morning to head over to Westmount, and she usually returned home by three forty-five in the afternoon. The only exceptions were Wednesdays, when she monitored Homework Help in the library after school, and the second Monday of every month, when there was an afternoon staff meeting. She didn't, as far as he could tell, date very often—or maybe not at all.

Which piqued his curiosity for two reasons: first, she was a beautiful woman, and second, she was new to Haven. Either of those factors would appeal to most of the single guys in town; the combination would prove almost irresistible. This led Jay to believe her presence at home most nights was a matter of choice. But why?

Was she involved with somebody back in California? Was she nursing a broken heart? Or was she simply not interested in any of the guys she'd met?

It wasn't in his nature to ignore an intrigue, but he didn't like being distracted by thoughts of a woman.

So rather than admit that he was, he pushed all thoughts of her out of his mind and focused on getting ready for work.

Alyssa turned off the water, grabbed a towel from the bar and briskly rubbed it over her body. She knew, without looking at the clock, that it was 7:00 a.m. She knew because she was a creature of habit who awakened every morning at six and had her shoes laced up, ready to head out the door, ten minutes later.

She wasn't a competitive runner—not like her sister, Cristina, had been. But she enjoyed challenging herself to go a little farther, a little faster. After too many years of being told to be careful, to slow down, because she was fragile and weak, she had a lot to prove—if only to herself.

She'd started running three years earlier, just a short jog at a moderate pace, to see if she could. And then she could do a little more—and a little faster. Now she was strong, she was fit and she was determined to live her life on her own terms.

She ran for herself. It wasn't really a secret, but it also wasn't something she'd shared with anyone else.

Until Jason Channing.

Somehow, eight weeks earlier, she'd acquired a running partner she didn't need or want. And despite her less-than-welcoming demeanor at the start, he'd continued to show up, until she'd found herself not just enjoying his company but looking forward to it.

But at the same time, being around her upstairs neighbor also left her feeling a little…unsettled.

Of course, if rumors were to be believed—and in the eight months she'd lived in Haven, she'd discovered that they usually were—he had a similar effect on most of the female population in town. Because not only was he unbelievably handsome and charming, he was educated, motivated and rich. Not that he flaunted his wealth. In fact, it was only through a conversation with Mrs. Powell, the resident of 1A, that she'd discovered he owned the triplex they all lived in.

Still, it had taken her a while to accept that the cause of her unsettled feeling was most likely physical attraction. But what woman wouldn't feel some kind of stirring in her blood when she was around a good-looking guy? And Jason Channing was undoubtedly that. Referred to as "Charming" by the women in town, he was six feet tall with broad shoulders, dark hair, deep blue eyes, a square jaw and an easy smile that never failed to make Alyssa's toes curl inside her running shoes.

So although she couldn't deny that she was attracted, she was thankfully smart enough to realize that he was way out of her league. And that was okay, because when it came to the dating game, she was content to sit in the bleachers and watch others play.

Someday she might be ready to suit up and hit the field, but after so many years of being "coached" by her doctors and parents, she just wanted to call her own plays for a while. Which was why she'd finally moved away from the well-meaning but stifling attention of her family.

Eight months later, Renata Cabrera still hadn't let up in her campaign to get her youngest daughter to come home. Her latest effort, begun when Alyssa was home for the Christmas holidays, had been a reintroduction to Diego Garcia. He was "handsome and single" as her mother had promised, but Alyssa simply wasn't interested.

Unfortunately, Renata refused to believe it, and Alyssa couldn't remember the last conversation she'd had with her mother without some mention of Diego. Most recently Renata had suggested that he might be traveling to Nevada to help his cousin, who lived in Elko and had recently split from his girlfriend, move out of their shared apartment and into his own. Alyssa hated to think that her mother had encouraged Diego to make the trip—or to think that she had any kind of personal interest in him—but she couldn't disregard either possibility.

With her travel mug of coffee in one hand and car keys in the other, Alyssa had just stepped onto the driveway when her phone rang. Only one person ever called her early in the morning, so she didn't need to glance at the display to know who it was.

She unlocked the car door and set her coffee in the cup holder on the console before pulling the phone out of her purse and connecting the call. "*Buenos días*, Mama."

"I'm just calling to remind you that Diego's going to be in Nevada this weekend," her mother responded without preamble.

Alyssa closed her eyes and quietly banged her head against the open door. "I didn't realize those were firm plans."

"Then you weren't listening," Renata said.

"I'm working this weekend," she reminded her mother.

"You're working tonight," Renata acknowledged. "And Diego said he would stop by this Diggers' place so the two of you could make plans for when you're not working."

"I have another job, too," Alyssa said. "And test papers and lab reports to mark this weekend."

"You work too hard," her mother protested. "At the school all day and then a second job at night."

"Only two nights a week," she interjected to clarify the part-time status of her bartending job at the local watering hole.

"If you don't slow down, you're going to wear yourself out," Renata continued, as if she hadn't heard her.

Alyssa didn't bother to point out that her sister worked

a full-time job and then cared for a husband and son when she got home, and nobody worried that Cristina was going to wear herself out. All she said was "I'm fine, Mama."

"You need a break," Renata said. "And I think spending some time with Diego will fit the bill nicely."

"Diego's a nice guy," she began in an effort to appease her mother.

"From a good family," Renata pointed out. "And ready to settle down and start a family of his own."

Which was something Alyssa was definitely *not* ready to do. "Mama—"

"Would it be such a hardship to spend some time with an interesting and attractive single man?"

"Of course not," she acknowledged. "But—" she needed to firmly and finally extinguish any hopes her mother had of striking a romantic match between Alyssa and Diego "—the truth is, I've been seeing somebody here."

Except that it wasn't the truth—it was a blatant lie.

But desperate times called for desperate measures.

"You've been seeing someone?" her mother echoed, not bothering to hide her skepticism.

"That's right," she confirmed.

*Lied.*

*Again.*

"And why am I only hearing about this now?" Renata challenged.

"I didn't want to jinx the relationship by talking about it too soon."

But apparently she didn't mind going to hell, which was certainly her destination after she added more falsehoods and untruths to the conversation.

"Well, this puts me in an extremely awkward position, Alyssa," Renata said. "If I'd known about this…relationship…I would not have encouraged Diego to look you up while he's in town."

She didn't bother to point out that Elko was a different town in a different county. "Maybe it's not too late to get in touch with him and recommend he change his plans," she suggested hopefully.

"Unfortunately, it is," her mother said. "He's already in Nevada, so I'm just going to trust that, when you see him tonight, you'll treat him as you would any friend visiting from out of town."

"Of course," Alyssa murmured, her mind once again scrambling. "But now I really do have to go, so I'm not late for work."

"Okay," Renata said. "But don't forgot to call Nicolas next week to wish him a happy birthday."

"I won't forget," she promised, already looking forward to talking to her almost-five-year-old nephew—because although he always told her he missed her, *he* never tried to guilt her into moving back to California. "Goodbye, Mama. *Te quiero.*"

After her mother had said goodbye, too, Alyssa disconnected the call and sighed wearily. "I'm going to hell."

"I'm not a priest, but I'm willing to listen to your confession, if it would help."

She jolted at the sound of Jason's voice behind her, then pressed a hand to her racing heart as she turned to face him. Of course, seeing him now, freshly showered and shaven, her heart raced even faster.

"Sorry to startle you," he said.

"It's okay," she said. "I didn't expect— You don't usually leave for work this early, do you?"

"No," he admitted. "And you don't usually leave this late."

She glanced at the clock display on her phone and winced. "You're right."

"I don't want to hold you up any longer, but I'm curious to hear why you think you're going to hell."

"Because I lied to my mother," she confided.

"A big fat lie or a little white lie?" he asked.

"I told her that I had a boyfriend."

"You don't?"

She shook her head. "No. The last date I had—and I'm not sure it even counts as a date—was the staff Christmas party, December 22."

She'd attended the event with Troy Hartwell, the biology teacher. He'd had a little too much to drink and misinterpreted her level of interest, forcing Alyssa to demonstrate some of the moves she'd learned in the self-defense course her mother had implored her to take before she moved away from home.

"Any particular reason for the dating hiatus?" Jason wondered.

"Not really," she said. "I just have other priorities right now—including a test for my senior calculus class this morning."

Jason took the hint. "Well, good luck with that," he said, moving around to the driver's side of his truck and climbing behind the wheel.

She waved as he drove away, then decided that her mother's ongoing matchmaking efforts meant it was time for her to implement plan B.

## Chapter Two

"The warehouse. Eighteen hundred hours. Tonight."

Jay shifted his attention from the spreadsheet on his computer to Carter Ford, his best friend of nearly two decades and now his right-hand man at Jason Channing Enterprises. Carter stood in the doorway of Jay's office, which also served as the staff lounge and lunch room of Adventure Village.

He glanced at the papers spread out on his desk and, with sincere reluctance, shook his head. "It's going to take me forever to sort this stuff out."

"What stuff?" Carter asked.

"Invoices to pay, booking requests to log and emails to answer."

His friend crossed the concrete floor and dropped into one of the visitors' chairs, then lifted his feet onto the seat of another. "Isn't that Naomi's job?"

"It was supposed to be," he admitted, scrubbing his

hands over his face. "Until I realized that we were two months behind on our insurance payments and we missed out on the opportunity to host a corporate team-building exercise for fifty people because the email was ignored."

The missed opportunity was an annoyance; the potential loss of liability insurance could have shut down their business.

"I thought you'd set up preauthorized payments for the insurance," Carter said.

He nodded. "For the first six months, the payments were coming out of my personal account, to give the business a chance to turn a profit. Then the automatic debits were supposed to be switched over to the Adventure Village account, but Naomi didn't send the paperwork to the bank."

Carter swore. "Tell me again why we're giving her a paycheck every two weeks."

"She got her last one today," Jay told him.

His friend's brows winged upward. "You fired your cousin?"

"Yeah."

"Your aunt's gonna be so pissed."

"Yeah," he said again, already braced for the fallout.

But he trusted that, if it came down to a family battle, his father would be on his side. Because Benjamin Channing had been the one to urge Jay to find a job for his cousin at Adventure Village so that Ben wouldn't have to make a position for her at Blake Mining. Naomi had an extensive work history, but she'd never managed to hold on to any job for very long. "And while I'm not opposed to nepotism, I am opposed to incompetence—and that's why I've got to deal with this paperwork," he explained to his friend.

"C'mon, Jay, you can take a break for a few hours," Carter urged.

"Maybe tomorrow night," he suggested.

"It has to be tonight," his friend insisted.

"Why?"

"Because it's our first anniversary."

Though he was aware of the significance of the date and knew his friend was referring to the business, he couldn't resist joking, "So where are my flowers?"

"The shop was out of yellow roses," Carter bantered back. "And I know they're your favorite."

"Tell me you at least got a card."

"Mere words cannot express my feelings," his friend said.

Jay snorted.

"But I'll buy you a beer after paintball tonight," Carter offered. "And we'll toast to year one."

"And account ledgers written entirely in black ink," Jay added, sitting back in his chair.

He believed in working hard and playing hard, and he considered himself lucky that there was a fair amount of overlap between work and play for the CEO of Adventure Village, Haven's family friendly recreational playground.

When he'd bought his first property—two acres of dry, dusty terrain that included an old abandoned shoe factory—several of the townsfolk had scratched their heads as they tried to figure out why he would throw his money away. Few people gave him credit for having a plan; even fewer believed he might have a viable one, especially when he acquired the undeveloped parcel directly behind the old factory.

He didn't talk about his project except with those who'd been chosen to work on the development. Because Jay knew that the best way to create buzz about what he was doing was to say nothing. The less people knew, the more they tended to speculate—and then share their speculation with friends and neighbors, who passed it on to other friends and neighbors.

When Adventure Village opened, he'd hoped all the doubters and naysayers and everyone else would understand that the land he'd purchased was an investment—not just in Jason's future, but that of the whole town. As one of only three cities in all of Nevada where gambling was illegal, Haven saw a steady exodus of residents to the casinos in neighboring areas on evenings and weekends. And who could blame them when there was no action in their hometown?

But now the residents of Haven had another option. And not only were fewer people heading out of town on weekends, there were more people heading *to* Haven from other places.

Jay understood that part of the draw, at least in the beginning, was the newness and novelty of his facility. In a state where most people came to fritter away their money at the tables or in the bordellos, a facility that offered a variety of wholesome physical activities for all ages was an anomaly—and week after week, that anomaly was adding to his status as one of the wealthiest men in Haven.

And that was definitely cause for celebration.

"What's the plan?"

"Assassins," Carter immediately replied, proving that he'd already given the matter some thought. Or maybe it was just that Assassins was always his game of choice whenever they geared up and took to the field.

"Who's in?"

"Kevin, Matt, Nat, Hayley, me and you."

Jay looked at the papers on his desk again.

"You started this business because you wanted to have fun," his friend reminded him.

"Yeah," he admitted. "But I didn't realize that fun could be so much work."

"And that's why you need a break."

"Why can't that break be tomorrow night?" he wondered.

"Because after the game, Kev wants to head over to Diggers' to put his moves on the hot new bartender, and she doesn't work Saturdays."

"Kev has no moves," Jay noted. "And what he thinks is hot is usually only lukewarm."

"You're right about the moves," his friend agreed. "But his description of the bartender was actually 'sizzling.'"

"Now you have my attention."

Carter grinned.

Jay decided the unpaid and undocumented invoices would still be there tomorrow.

Alyssa loved her job at Westmount High School. Teaching was her pride and her passion, and helping young minds understand scientific laws and mathematic formulas was incredibly fulfilling. But despite a full timetable and the prep and marking to be completed outside of regular school hours, when she walked out of her classroom at the end of the day, she found that she had a lot of free time on her hands.

So she'd looked for opportunities to meet people and get involved in the community. She joined a book club, but the required readings and once-a-month meetings did little to fill her empty nights. She tried a pottery class but had more luck throwing her misshapen vessels into the trash than throwing clay on the wheel. She tried to teach herself to knit but got the needles hopelessly tangled— not just in the wool she'd bought for her project, but in the sweater she'd been wearing. As a result, she'd filled most of her empty hours through the long winter binge-watching Netflix.

Then one day, when she was picking up a few groceries at The Trading Post, she overheard Frieda Zimmerman (whose husband was the local mechanic and tow truck operator) tell Thomas Mann (the owner of Mann's Theater) that her niece Erika had run off to Vegas to be a dancer. Alyssa hadn't been paying too much attention to their conversation, but her attention was snagged when Mr. Mann commented that Diggers' was going to be short a bartender. Because that was a job Alyssa had some experience with, having worked part-time at a campus bar while she was in college.

Her parents had acknowledged the value of their youngest daughter gaining some work experience and contributing to the cost of her education, but they hadn't approved of the late hours or the work environment. It was the first time Alyssa hadn't backed down in the face of their opposition, and although the job had been physically demanding, she'd enjoyed the work—and the chance to forget about her studies and everything else for a while.

Even on Friday nights, Diggers' didn't draw a crowd comparable to a college bar in Irvine, but Alyssa was eager for something—*anything*—to fill some empty hours. Duke Hawkins had been wary about hiring a schoolteacher to tend his bar, but as she was the only applicant with any actual experience, he'd agreed to give her a chance. In only a few short weeks, she'd earned regular shifts on Tuesday and Friday nights.

Sunday through Thursday, there was only one bartender on duty, but on weekends, there were two scheduled with overlapping shifts. Alyssa worked from seven until midnight and Skylar Gilmore came in at eight and stayed until closing. Sky was a couple years younger than Alyssa, but she'd been working part-time at the bar since she was of age and was now a master of the subtle flirtation that kept customers coming back without expecting anything more from the woman who filled their glasses.

Everyone in town knew Sky as the youngest daughter of David Gilmore, owner and operator of the Circle G— reputedly the biggest and most prosperous cattle ranch in Nevada. Few people knew that she was working toward her master's degree in psychology. She was also open and warm and funny, and she knew everything there was to know about Diggers' regular customers—and most of the less regular patrons, too.

Sky was the third of four kids. Her older sister was an attorney married to the local sheriff, Reid Davidson. In February, Katelyn and Reid had added a baby girl to their family, and proud Aunt Sky was always ready to pull out her phone and share recent pictures of her niece, Tessa. Liam, the second oldest, currently worked at the Circle G with his father and brother, though he'd recently purchased the abandoned Stagecoach Inn with the intention of renovating and reopening it as a boutique hotel and spa.

This plan had caused some tension with his father, who apparently insisted that Gilmores were ranchers, not innkeepers, which led to Liam spending less time at the Circle G and more at Diggers'—which was how Alyssa got to know him. Caleb, the youngest, seemed content to work on the ranch, though Sky remarked that he hadn't been truly happy since a former girlfriend moved out of town a few years back.

"Liam said to tell you that one of the bulls broke through the fence bordering the south pasture," Sky said when she joined Alyssa behind the bar Friday night.

"Does that mean he's not coming in tonight?"

"He's coming in," her coworker assured her. "But he's going to be late."

"Oh. Okay," she said, though she knew that if he was *too* late, her plan B would fall apart.

"What he didn't tell me," Sky continued, as if thinking aloud, "is why it was so important for him to show up tonight—or why you would have any interest in his plans."

"It's a long story," Alyssa warned.

"We've got time—this place won't get busy for at least another hour."

So Alyssa told Sky about Diego's impending visit to Haven. Ordinarily, she'd have no qualms about spending time with a family friend visiting from out of town, except that her mother had been less than subtle in her efforts to facilitate a romance between her youngest daughter and the nephew of her best friend, and Alyssa wasn't the least bit interested.

"Is he a jerk?" Sky asked.

"No."

"Unattractive?"

"No." Because although she wasn't attracted to him, she could appreciate that he had a certain appeal.

"Unemployed?"

"No," she said again. "In fact, he works as a project engineer in the aerospace industry."

"So why aren't you interested?" Sky wondered.

"Because I don't want to date anyone right now—especially not someone handpicked by my mother for the sole purpose of enticing me to move back to California."

"How does my brother figure into any of this?"

"He had the misfortune of being here Tuesday night when my mother called to tell me about Diego's potential travel plans. And he suggested that the only sure way to stop her from setting me up with someone from home was to tell her I'm dating someone here. So—" she looked at Sky, trying to gauge her friend's reaction "—Liam's going to be my pretend boyfriend tonight."

Her friend's brows lifted. "Pretend, huh?"

"Pretend," Alyssa said firmly.

"Oh," Sky said, sounding disappointed. "For a minute, I thought this story might be as good as the sexy book I stayed up all night reading."

"Maybe I can borrow it when you're done, because the only romance I want these days is in the pages of a novel," Alyssa told her.

"Why's that?"

"Because I like my life the way it is—uncomplicated by the expectations of a man."

"Most men are simple creatures driven by simple desires to eat, sleep and have sex." Sky grinned. "Although not necessarily in that order."

Alyssa's experiences with the male gender were too limited for her to be able to contradict her friend's assessment. Instead, she said, "And I have no desire to cook so that a man can eat, or make up the bed for him to sleep on."

"I noticed that you didn't dis the sex," Sky said, her tone contemplative.

"My experience in that area is limited," she admitted.

"How limited?"

"Let's just say I really don't get what all the fuss is about."

"Then you haven't been with the right kind of guy," her friend said. "And it's probably a good thing you only want Liam to be a pretend boyfriend."

"Now you've piqued my curiosity," Alyssa said.

"I love both of my brothers dearly, but Liam is…" Sky paused, as if searching for the right words to express what she was thinking. "He's not always considerate of a woman's emotions." She smiled wryly. "Sometimes he's not even cognizant of them."

"So if I was going to fall for one of the Gilmore boys, I should set my sights on Caleb?" Alyssa joked.

Her friend shook her head. "Except that my younger brother, though inherently more compassionate, is completely emotionally unavailable."

"Then I guess it's a good thing I'm not looking to fall for anyone," she noted.

"Those not looking are most likely to fall," Sky warned.

"I'm not concerned."

"How long have you been in Haven?" her friend asked as she began to unload a tray of glasses.

"Eight months," she answered.

"How many dates have you had in that time?"

"Two," she admitted.

"Two dates with the same guy or two different guys?" Sky continued to multitask as she interrogated her.

"Two different guys," Alyssa clarified. "Neither of which I wanted a second date with."

"Sex?"

She shook her head.

Sky gave Alyssa her full attention now. "You haven't had sex in *eight months*?"

Alyssa's cheeks flushed. "It's actually been a little bit longer than that." Actually, it had been *a lot* longer than that, but she wasn't ready to admit to her friend that she was a twenty-six-year-old virgin.

"You haven't met anyone in that time who's made you think 'yeah, I could get naked with him'?" Sky asked.

Even as she shook her head again, an image of Jason Channing filled her mind and heated her blood. Whenever she was around her upstairs neighbor and current running partner, *feelings*—unfamiliar and unwelcome—stirred inside her. Those feelings sometimes made it difficult to remember that she was happy living her own life and definitely not looking for romance. And even if she was, it would be a mistake to glance in his direction.

"No," she said in answer to Sky's question.

But then he walked right out of her thoughts and into the bar, and her defective heart skipped a beat.

He wasn't alone. Of course "Charming" wasn't alone on a Friday night. He was with a woman—blonde, beautiful, built. No, he was with *two* women. The second was a little taller, with darker hair, but no less beautiful. A second man followed the second woman, and they headed directly for one of the booths.

A double date, Alyssa guessed.

Then two more guys came in and squeezed into the booth, too.

Or maybe just a group of friends, she allowed.

Alyssa tore her gaze away from them to glance at the clock. Because as nice as Jason Channing was to look at, he wasn't the man she wanted to see right now.

In fact, he wasn't a man she could let herself want at all.

## Chapter Three

As Jay made his way to the bar, he watched Alyssa give a smile to her customer along with his change. Her attention shifted, and though it might have been his imagination, he thought her smile widened when she recognized him.

"So you're the one," he said to her.

"The one what?" she asked.

"My friend Kevin insisted that we come here tonight to check out the hot new bartender," he explained.

She automatically glanced toward the table where his friends were seated, suggesting that she'd seen them enter the bar. "Setting aside the accuracy of that description for the moment, I hope he didn't make the suggestion in front of your new girlfriend."

"My— Oh." He looked over his shoulder. "Which one did you think was my girlfriend?"

She shrugged. "Either. Both."

"I'm flattered… I think. But no, Nat and Hayley are friends and employees."

"Is the boss buying the first round tonight?" she prompted.

Although there were servers who circulated around the floor, taking orders and delivering drinks, it wasn't unusual for customers to order directly from the bartender.

"I am," Jay confirmed. "Two bottles of Icky, one Wild Horse, a gin and tonic, one Maker's Mark, neat, and a Coke."

She turned to reach into the beer fridge for the bottles he'd requested, providing him with a nice view of her perfectly shaped backside.

"So what made you take up bartending?" he asked, his attention focusing on the chunky, lopsided heart-shaped pendant that dangled between her breasts when she turned back again.

"Too much time on my hands," she confided, deftly uncapping the bottles.

He lifted his eyes to her face again. "Did you lose your teaching job?"

"Of course not."

"Then what you really meant to say was too many lonely nights," he teased.

"I'm not lonely," she denied, scooping ice into a tall glass. "But I spend a lot of time alone and I thought this would be a good way to meet people."

"How's that working out so far?"

She smiled as she filled the glass from the soda gun. "The tips are good."

He chuckled.

"Aside from that," she continued as she poured the bourbon into an old-fashioned glass, "I've learned there are three types of guys who come into a bar."

"What are those types?" he asked curiously.

"Type one are the regulars who might be genuinely nice guys, but their closest and longest relationships are with the bottle," she explained as she scooped more ice into a highball.

"Type two comes in looking to meet a woman, but he doesn't have any interest in getting to know her beyond the most basic exchange of information for the sole purpose of getting her into bed." She added a shot of gin, then squeezed a wedge of lime into the glass.

"Type three is almost worse." She added the tonic, another wedge of lime and a stir stick. "He seems like a good guy, and he's usually with a girl who thinks so, too, but the whole time he's with her, he's scoping out the area for other females."

"I'd suggest that there's also a fourth type," Jay said. "The guy who comes in for a drink with his friends and maybe to flirt with a pretty girl."

"Maybe," she acknowledged, a little dubiously.

"And then there's Carter," he said as his friend joined him at the bar—ostensibly to help him carry the drinks back to their table.

"Hello, Carter," she said, greeting the other man with a friendly smile.

"For once in his life, Kevin was right," Carter remarked, winking boldly at Alyssa.

Jay shook his head. "Type two," he told her. "Not beyond reform, but risky."

Alyssa nodded as she punched the drinks into the register. "Got it."

Carter scowled. "What does that mean? What's a type two?"

"It means that you're *not* going to hit on the bartender—who also happens to be my neighbor," he said firmly.

His friend's gaze shifted from him to Alyssa and back again. "You live next to this stunning creature and you've never invited me over to meet her?"

"And this is him pretending that he's not hitting on you," Jay remarked as he passed some bills across the counter to Alyssa.

She laughed. "Well, I'm flattered," she said.

"Let me know when you want to be *not* pretend hit on," Carter told her, picking up several of the drinks to take them back to their table.

Jay shook his head to decline the change she offered.

Her smile slipped, replaced by an expression of concern. "Ohmygod."

He craned his neck, looking behind him. "What happened?"

"That's what I was going to ask you," she said.

"What do you mean?"

She lifted a hand to touch his face, her fingers brushing lightly over the stubble on his jaw—and the bruise that throbbed beneath the skin.

"Oh, that," he said, wondering how it was that her cautious touch was so unexpectedly arousing. "Matt caught me with my shield up."

"Huh?"

"Paintball," he explained.

"Boys and their toys," she mused, letting her hand drop away.

His skin continued to tingle where she'd touched him.

Or maybe that was just the bruise.

Yeah, it was definitely the bruise, he decided as he picked up the remaining drinks and walked away from the bar. Because he definitely wasn't letting himself get involved with the girl next door.

\* \* \*

"You calling dibs?" Carter asked when Jay rejoined his friends at their table.

"Dibs on what?" Matt Hutchinson wanted to know.

"Of course I'm not calling dibs," Jay said.

"The bartender," Natalya Vasilek answered Matt's question.

"If anyone's calling dibs, it's me," Kevin Dawson declared. "I saw her first."

"No, you didn't," Carter told him. "Because the 'hot new bartender' is a friend and neighbor of our CEO."

Kevin swore.

"But he's not calling dibs," Matt reminded them all.

"Maybe because he likes and respects the woman too much to talk about her as if she was an object up for grabs," Hayley MacDowell said sharply.

"Whatever Jay's reasons," Kevin insisted, "if he's not calling dibs, *I* am."

"No one is calling dibs on Alyssa," Jay said in a tone that brooked no argument.

Carter tipped his bottle to his lips but kept his gaze on his friend, silently assessing.

Conversation moved on to other topics, including a rehashing of all the highlights of their recent game. As they talked, their glasses and bottles emptied.

"I think Alyssa's the real reason you broke up with Renee," Carter said to Jay when the play-by-play had begun to lag.

"I broke up with Renee because she ranked below my business and my friends on my list of priorities," he replied.

"That might be true," Nat allowed. "But that doesn't explain why you keep looking at the bartender."

He dragged his gaze away from Alyssa.

"And the Master Assassin strikes again," Hayley noted.

"Who's got the next round?" Jay asked, holding up his empty glass.

"I think it's my turn," Hayley said, pushing away from the table.

"I'm out," Matt said. "I've gotta get home to Carrie."

Kevin made a sound like a whip being cracked.

Their soon-to-be-married friend was unperturbed. "Yeah, it's a real drag, being engaged to a gorgeous woman with whom I share mutual interests, stimulating conversation and really hot sex."

"I'll give you a hand," Nat said to Hayley, no doubt eager for an excuse to leave the three remaining men at the table.

When they returned with the next round of drinks, conversation shifted again to more neutral topics.

A short while later, Kevin left with Hayley, because they were headed in the same direction. Then Carter and Nat headed out together. Jay knew that he should make his way home, too. Weekends were the busiest time at Adventure Village, and he had the early-morning shift the next day—including two birthday parties on-site.

But he stayed where he was, sipping his Coke and wondering about the discovery that his neighbor and the hot new bartender were one and the same.

Though pouring drinks kept her hands busy, Alyssa's gaze kept shifting between the clock and the door—and, occasionally, the table where Jason was sitting with his friends. Where he remained after his friends had gone.

Sky bumped her hip. "Should we update our earlier conversation?"

"About what?" Alyssa looked at the clock again.

"Your claim that you have yet to meet someone with whom you want to get naked. Because while you're acting as if you're not watching Jason Channing, he's acting as if he's not watching you."

She shook her head. "Jason's my neighbor."

"That could be convenient," her friend said.

"Have you heard anything from Liam?" she asked, eager to change the topic of conversation—and for Sky's brother to make his promised appearance.

Now Sky glanced at the clock and frowned. "No, I haven't. And I didn't expect him to be *this* late."

The only consolation for Alyssa was that Diego was late, too. Or maybe he wasn't coming. She mentally crossed her fingers that she could get so lucky.

"I'll see if I can reach him on his cell," Sky said.

"Thanks."

She looked at the clock again.

Nine twenty-eight.

Sky shook her head as she tucked her phone back into her pocket before heading to the other end of the bar to refill Gavin Virga's drink.

Alyssa sighed.

"Is something wrong?"

She jolted at the sound of his voice so close, then laughed as she pressed a hand to the heart that was hammering inside her chest.

"I seem to have a habit of startling you," Jason apologized.

"It's okay," she said. "My mind was just somewhere else."

"I can't imagine anywhere more interesting than here," he deadpanned.

She laughed again. "Did you want something to drink?"

He shook his head. "I noticed that you've been watching the door."

"I guess I have been," she admitted.

"Waiting for someone?" He straddled an empty stool.

"Sort of."

"How can you 'sort of' be waiting for someone?"

"Well, there's one person I'm hoping will come through the door and another I'm hoping won't," she explained.

"Now I'm intrigued," he said.

Over his shoulder, she saw a familiar figure walk into the bar and swore under her breath.

Or maybe the curse wasn't as restrained as she thought, because Jason's brows lifted—a silent question that she didn't have time to answer. Because Diego had spotted her, too, and was moving purposefully toward her.

And though Jason hadn't been her first choice, she decided that if she could have a fantasy romance with any man of her choosing, there wasn't anyone more fantasy worthy than her handsome upstairs neighbor.

"I'll explain later," she promised as growing desperation pushed aside both rational thought and common sense. "For now, will you please just go with it?"

"Go with—"

She didn't let him finish the question before she leaned across the bar and kissed him.

If this was "it," Jason decided as Alyssa's mouth moved over his, he could definitely go with it. For now and as long as she wanted, because her lips were soft and warm and seductively persuasive.

He'd be lying if he said that he hadn't thought about kissing her, because she was the type of woman that any red-blooded man would be attracted to. But he also knew that it wasn't always a good idea to act on an attraction—such as when the woman who stirred his blood was a friend, co-worker or neighbor. Alyssa checked off two of those boxes, so no matter how much his hormones sat up and begged for attention whenever she was around—and there was no denying that they did—he'd mostly managed to ignore them.

There was no hope of ignoring them now.

She smelled so good…tasted even better.

And he wished there wasn't eighteen inches of polished walnut between them, so that he could put his arms around her and haul her against his body. He settled for circling her wrists with his hands. His thumbs rubbed over her pulse points, finding evidence that her heart was racing as fast as his own.

"I think that should do it." She whispered the words against his lips before she eased away.

*Do what?* he wondered, noting that her mouth was moist and swollen from their kiss, her cheeks flushed.

But before he could catch his breath to ask the question aloud, someone spoke from behind him.

"I heard this was a friendly establishment," the male voice remarked. "Do all customers get that kind of attention?"

The color in her cheeks deepened. "Diego…um…hi." Then she seemed to gather her thoughts to respond to his question. "And, uh, no."

"You must be someone special, then," the man she'd referred to as Diego remarked, his narrowed gaze focused on Jay.

"Very special," Alyssa chimed in quickly. "Jason is… my boyfriend."

Though Jay instinctively chafed against the word, the silent plea in her eyes begged him not to contradict her claim. Recalling her promise of an explanation later, he decided to go with it—at least for now.

"And you would be?" Jay prompted the other man.

Alyssa jumped in again. "This is Diego Garcia, a family friend from California."

"Well, any friend of Alyssa's is a friend of mine," he said.

Diego shook his proffered hand, squeezing more firmly than was warranted.

"You're a long way from home," Jay commented.

"I'm visiting a cousin in Elko," Diego said. "And since I was going to be so close, Renata suggested that I stop in to say hi to her daughter."

"And now you have," he said pointedly.

Diego nodded and turned his attention back to Alyssa. "If you're not working tomorrow night, maybe we could have dinner together," he suggested.

"I'm not working," she admitted, glancing at Jay, those melted chocolate eyes pleading. "But—"

"But we already have plans for tomorrow night," he finished for her.

"Plans that can't be changed to accommodate a friend from back home?" Diego directed the question at Alyssa.

"Unfortunately, yes," Jay responded. "You see, it's our three-month anniversary tomorrow and I have a very special evening planned."

"How about lunch, then?" the other man offered as an alternative.

"Sorry," he interjected, though the invitation clearly hadn't been directed at—or even intended to include—him. "But we're tied up for the whole weekend."

"And I'm heading back Sunday morning," Diego admitted.

"Well, I hope you enjoy your visit with your cousin and have a safe trip back," Alyssa said, clearly eager for the man to be on his way.

Jay knew that would probably be for the best, but he couldn't deny a certain curiosity about Diego's connection to his neighbor. And since Alyssa herself was rather tight-lipped whenever he asked her about her previous life in California, he decided that this was too good an opportunity to pass up.

"But since you're here now," he said to the other man, "why don't you let me buy you a drink?"

## Chapter Four

*W*hat was he doing?

Alyssa frowned at Jason, silently communicating her annoyance.

She couldn't imagine Diego saying yes, but still—what could have possessed her pretend boyfriend to make such an offer? She held her breath as Diego glanced at his watch, shrugged.

"I wouldn't mind a cup of coffee before I make the drive back," he decided.

"Make that two cups, honey bear," Jason said to her.

*Honey bear?*

But of course, she couldn't object to his use of the term because she needed his help if her ploy was to succeed. Instead, she forced a smile. "Of course, sugar muffin. I was just about to make a fresh pot—I'll have Geena bring it over when it's ready."

Though his brows lifted, a smile tugged at the corners

of his mouth before he turned away to guide Diego to a vacant table.

"Sugar muffin?" Sky echoed quizzically.

"It was the first thing that came to mind," Alyssa admitted.

"I can't believe you're fake cheating on my brother with someone called 'sugar muffin,'" her coworker remarked.

"Your brother stood me up," Alyssa pointed out in her defense.

"He was late," Sky acknowledged, pretending to be miffed. "And you didn't wait half an hour to throw yourself into another man's arms."

"Actually, I waited thirty-three minutes," she said. "Desperate times and all that."

But even as her words justified her actions, her heart—still racing from that kiss—worried that she might have made a very big mistake.

Sky glanced at the table where Jason and Diego were seated as she continued to mix drinks. "He's actually kind of cute."

"Jason?"

"No!" Sky said immediately. Vehemently. "Diego."

Objectively speaking, her friend was right. But Alyssa was more curious about Sky's reaction to her question about Jason. "Do you have a history with Jason Channing that I should know about?"

Sky shook her head. "Not personally."

"Impersonally?"

Her friend chuckled. "No. It's just that I'm a Gilmore and he's a Blake—or rather, his mother was a Blake."

"I'm still not following," she admitted.

"You don't know about the feud?"

"What feud?"

Sky shook her head, but before she could explain, Margot—one of the waitresses—came up to the bar with an order of drinks for a party table in the restaurant, and Sky turned her attention to filling it.

While she was busy doing that, Alyssa grabbed a bus pan to clear some of the now empty tables.

Jason and Diego were still chatting, and though she was admittedly curious about the topic of their conversation, she wasn't worried. She'd made her point to Diego. Now he could go back to Elko—and ultimately to Irvine—cured of any notion that there was a future for them together.

She sprayed and wiped a table, then turned and found herself face-to-face with her mother's best friend's favorite nephew.

"I wanted to say goodbye before I headed out," Diego said to her.

"Oh. Okay." She tightened her grip on the bus pan as he leaned over to kiss her on one cheek, then the other.

"It was good to see you, even for a couple of minutes, Alyssa."

"You, too." And now that she knew he was leaving, she managed to say the words with a believable amount of sincerity.

Or maybe she was *too* believable, because he tried again. "You're sure you don't have any free time this weekend?"

She glanced at the table where Jason was still sitting, watching them, and shook her head. "I don't know what plans Jason has made—" which was the absolute truth "—but if he says we're booked, we're booked."

"I guess I'll see you in July, then."

The expression on her face must have matched the blankness of her mind, because he smiled, and she realized that Sky was right—he was kind of cute. But she wasn't attracted to him in the least.

"Your parents' anniversary party," Diego reminded her. "I assume you'll be home for that?"

"Oh, yes. Of course," she agreed.

"Then I'll see you there."

She exhaled a long, grateful sigh of relief when he finally turned away and headed out the door—crossing paths with Liam Gilmore on his way in.

Sky's brother glanced toward the bar, his gaze searching. Looking for Alyssa. He found her and was at her side with a few quick strides.

"I'm late," he acknowledged, his breathless tone suggesting that he'd raced to get there.

"It's okay," she told him.

He took the bus pan from her and set it on the table. "You're too understanding," he said. "And I'm so lucky that you're mine."

Then he pulled her into his arms and kissed her.

Sharing a public kiss with Jason Channing had drawn more attention than Alyssa wanted. Now, barely more than an hour later, she was kissing Liam Gilmore in the same bar—with Jason Channing watching!

She pulled away. "Stop. Please."

"What's wrong?"

"What's wrong is that you're making a move on my girl," Jason said.

Liam scowled at the other man. "Excuse me?"

Jason slid an arm across her shoulders. "Honey bear, you said you were going to tell him that you'd finally found a real man."

Liam's eyes narrowed dangerously.

Alyssa stepped between the two men. "Diego was here and you weren't," she explained to Liam. "So I tagged Jason to fill in."

"There was no one else around?" Liam's tone was petulant.

"Only Jason and Gavin Virga," she said, naming the octogenarian ophthalmologist who was a Friday night regular.

"So why'd you pick *him*?" he asked again, glaring at Jason.

Alyssa nudged Liam toward the bar. "Go ask your sister to pour you a beer," she suggested.

He did so, but only after shooting one last narrow-eyed stare at Jason.

"I appreciate you pinch-hitting tonight," she said to Jason. "But now that Diego's gone, you can go, too."

"I haven't paid for the coffee."

"I did."

"Why?"

She shrugged. "I figured it was the least I could do to thank you for playing along."

His gaze dropped to her mouth, lingered. And when his lips started to curve, as if he was remembering the kiss they'd shared, her own started to tingle.

She pressed them firmly together and reminded herself that "Charming" had probably kissed most of the women in Haven at one time or another, and she shouldn't make the mistake of thinking that one spontaneous lip-lock had made any kind of impression on him.

"It wasn't much of a hardship," he assured her.

She picked up the bus pan again. "I've got to, uh, get this back to the kitchen."

He didn't object as she slipped past him.

The dishwasher took the pan from her with a nod of thanks, but Alyssa hid in the kitchen for another minute— just long enough to catch her breath and give her heart a chance to beat normally again.

It was just a kiss.

A kiss that had meant less than nothing to both of them. And yet…

She lifted a hand to her mouth.

And yet she'd felt so much in those few seconds that their lips had been connected. More than she'd ever felt from just a kiss. More than she'd ever felt with any other man.

"Alyssa?"

She started, her hand dropping from her lips as she turned to Sky. "Um, yeah. I'll be right out."

"Actually, I was going to tell you that you could take off early, if you want," her friend said. "Most of the tables are empty now and there are only a few stragglers left at the bar."

"Are you sure you don't mind?"

"I'm sure. And you've had a rather…eventful night already," Sky said, her tone tinged with amusement.

"That's one word for it," she agreed. "But I should talk to your brother before I go."

"Liam's cool—it's the other one who looked as if he was going to pop a vein in his head when he saw my brother kiss you."

"Jason?"

"For a moment, I thought fists were going to fly—and then I would've had to ban my own brother from the bar for a year."

It was a harsh punishment, but one Duke insisted be meted out to anyone who dared to throw a punch inside his establishment. Which might be why, in the eight months she'd lived in Haven, Alyssa had never heard about anyone fighting inside Diggers'—although rumor had it that Doug Holland's bar privileges had been reinstated only at the end of January, a full year after he'd given Jerry Tate a black eye for suggesting that his wife was stepping out. Sky had given Alyssa the background on the situation, explaining that Jerry had clearly been baiting the other man, because anyone who knew Doug's wife knew there wasn't another man in town who would want her.

She followed Sky back out front, surprised to discover that Jason had again taken a seat at the bar.

"I didn't expect you'd still be here," she said, glancing warily toward the opposite end of the counter, where Liam was sipping a beer and chatting with his sister.

"What kind of a man would leave his beautiful girl-friend alone in a place like this on a Friday night?" he countered.

"The kind of man who isn't really dating the bartender," she suggested.

"But that's not what you wanted Diego to think, was it?"

"Diego's probably halfway back to Elko by now," she pointed out.

"Still, I figured I should stick around in case he came back."

"I think—I hope—he finally got the message tonight."

"I wouldn't count on it," Jason said. "You were sending out some pretty mixed signals."

"What do you mean?"

"First you kissed me, then you kissed Gilmore."

She managed a weak smile. "Yeah. It's a good thing that Diego had already left, because that might have been a little hard to explain."

"Try explaining it to me," he suggested.

"I think I'm going to need a glass of wine for that."

"Are you allowed to drink on the job?"

She smiled as she shook her head. "I meant at home—I'm finished for the night."

His brows lifted. "And you're inviting me to go home with you—after only one kiss?"

"I'm offering to continue the explanation someplace

where I can kick off my shoes and put my feet up," she clarified.

He rose from his seat as she made her way around the bar.

"I'd offer to give you a lift home," he said, "but I got a ride with my friends—and they all abandoned me."

"So instead you're asking me for a lift home?"

He flashed his usual bone-melting smile. "If it won't take you too far out of your way."

"Lucky for you, my car has a full tank of gas."

He should have left the bar with his friends.

If Jay had walked out with Carter or Kevin, he wouldn't have ended up kissing Alyssa. Because now that he'd kissed her, he couldn't stop thinking about it—and wanting to do it again.

At twenty-nine, he was old enough to have learned that he couldn't always get what he wanted. But as a bachelor and heir to the Blake Mining fortune, it wasn't a lesson that seemed to apply in his relationships with women. Even back in high school, girls had practically lined up for the privilege of dating him, and he hadn't wanted to say no to any of them.

It had taken some time—and the anonymity that came with being an unknown freshman at an out-of-state college—before he gained some perspective. He no longer hit on every attractive woman who crossed his path, he ensured that any woman he did go out with wasn't under the illusion that a few nights in his bed would lead to a ring on her finger and he'd concluded that certain relationships tipped the scales against personal involvement—which was why he didn't date friends, coworkers or neighbors.

Alyssa was the first woman in a long time who tempted him to break that rule.

Going back to her place—which was only one flight of

stairs below his own—was an effective reminder of the most important reason not to make a move on his neighbor. And still, that reminder didn't completely snuff out the temptation.

"You were going to tell me about your love-struck suitor," Jay said, stepping across the threshold into her apartment.

She'd never invited him into her place before, and he was suddenly conscious of the fact that he was in her personal living space. A passing thought that turned his mind in a direction he was trying not to go. So he stayed where he was, just inside the door, while she crossed through the living room to the kitchen, her heels clicking on the hardwood floor.

"I don't think he's love-struck so much as misguided." She took a glass from the cupboard and removed the stopper from a previously opened bottle of wine on the counter. "And that's my mother's fault." She held up the bottle to show him the label. "Do you want a glass?"

"Do you have any beer?" he asked.

She shook her head. "Sorry."

"Then I'll have what you're having," he said.

She poured a second glass, then picked up both and carried them toward the seating area.

"Are you going to come inside and drink it?" she asked, the hint of a smile tugging at the corners of her mouth and lighting her dark eyes. "Or would you prefer to have it by the door?"

He'd stayed where he was in order to put as much physical space as possible between them, as if that distance might somehow dull his awareness of her. "It's a nice door," he said.

"Similar to the one on your apartment, I'd guess."

"Similar," he agreed as he crossed the floor to join her, though he chose a deep leather chair rather than the sofa where she'd settled. "And having spent some time with Diego tonight, I can tell you that he's more than misguided. In fact, I'd say he's somewhere between seriously infatuated and head over heels."

"What was that about, anyway?" she demanded. "He was ready to turn around and walk out the door when you asked him to stay."

"It was…an impulse," he told her, because he wasn't entirely sure of the reason himself.

"Why?" She lifted her glass to her lips.

He shrugged. "Doesn't the definition of impulse preclude there being a reason?"

"Not necessarily."

"And anyway, you're the one who promised an explanation," he reminded her.

"You're right."

"Am I also right in assuming that what happened tonight is somehow connected to the conversation you had with your mother this morning—the one in which you lied about having a boyfriend?"

She nodded.

"And the reason you lied?" he prompted.

"Because of Diego." She sipped her wine. "No, that's not entirely true. Diego is only the most recent of my mother's matchmaking efforts."

"How many have there been?" he wondered.

"It seems as if there's a new one every time I go home," she told him. "At Thanksgiving it was Tony. At Christmas it was Evan—until she realized no progress was being made there and brought Diego in to celebrate the New Year with us."

"Is your mother a professional matchmaker?"

"No. She's a financial analyst, but trying to find the perfect man for me has become her latest hobby. Or maybe it's an obsession. But it's not because she wants to help me find the perfect guy—she just wants me to find a guy who will convince me to move back to California. And not only is Diego her best friend's favorite nephew, he lives in the same neighborhood as my parents."

"That kind of relative and geographic proximity is a definite red flag," he agreed. "You never want to get involved with somebody that you might run into on a regular basis after the relationship ends, because those encounters can be awkward and messy."

She studied him over the rim of her glass. "On the surface, that sounds like a valid argument—except for one thing."

"What's that?"

"It assumes that every potential relationship is doomed from the start."

"Have you ever had a relationship that didn't end?" he challenged.

"Since I just told you about my mother's efforts to find my perfect match, it's safe to assume you already know the answer to that question."

"There you go," Jay said.

She shook her head. "Just because I'm not in love—and not looking for love—doesn't mean that I don't believe it exists," she told him. "And I'm not going to let some artificial boundary determine who I can and cannot date."

Which prompted him to ask the question that had been nudging at his mind for the past two hours: "Is that why you kissed me?"

Alyssa stared at him, certain she couldn't have heard him correctly. "What did you just say?"

"I asked if you kissed me because you were tired of waiting for me to make a move."

His response did nothing to clarify his question, but only succeeded in flustering her almost as much as the kiss.

"I was *never* waiting for you to make a move," she assured him. "And when I kissed you—that wasn't me making a move, that was sheer desperation."

He frowned. "You're saying that you *don't* want to go out with me?"

"Ohmygod—no!" she said quickly, emphatically.

"By all means, take a minute to think about the question before you answer," he said drily.

She felt her cheeks burn. "I don't need a minute to think about it," she said. "I do *not* want to go out with you."

Okay, maybe she secretly thought he was the hottest guy she'd ever known, but he wasn't at all her type. Not that she had a type—but she was certain that he did. She'd seen him around town with different women on various occasions, and they were all tall, slender and blonde. Alyssa was five feet six inches—when she was wearing two-inch heels—and though she wasn't overweight, she was definitely more curvy than most of the women he'd dated, with dark hair and eyes that attested to her Mexican heritage.

"And seriously, what kind of question is that?" she demanded. "How massive is your ego that you'd think I was looking for an opportunity to get close to you?"

He just shrugged. "A lot of women in this town consider me to be a catch."

"I'm not interested in catching you—or anyone. I don't even want to play the game."

"So I really was just in the wrong place at the wrong time?"

"You really were," she confirmed.

But even as she spoke those words to reassure him, there was a part of her that wondered if she was wrong—and that he'd been in exactly the right place at the right time.

## Chapter Five

Jay heard voices in the hall and glanced up when Carter, Nat and Kevin came into the office together the next morning. They had a tray of coffee and box of pastries from The Daily Grind, and he held out his hand for his usual—large, black—desperate for the hit of caffeine to revive his sluggish brain. He peeled back the lid and lifted the cup to his mouth.

"Thanks," he said. "I really needed that this morning—I don't think I managed even four hours of sleep last night."

Carter opened the box of pastries and Jay's gaze zeroed in on the bear claw—at the same moment Kevin snatched it out of the box and bit into it.

"I thought the bear claw was mine."

"Did you?" his friend asked around a mouthful of sweet, fried dough. "It really sucks when someone else moves in and takes something you've had your eye on, doesn't it?"

Jay looked questioningly at his other friends. "Why do I get the impression this isn't about the bear claw?"

"Because it's about Alyssa," Nat said.

"What about Alyssa?" he asked cautiously.

Kevin's only response was to take another big bite of the pastry.

"When we were at The Daily Grind, we heard Megan Carmichael telling Kenzie Atkins that you were locking lips with the new bartender at Diggers' last night," Nat explained.

Jay shouldn't have been surprised. The Daily Grind wasn't just Haven's café and bakery, it was where the latest rumors were always as hot as the coffee.

"It's not what you think," he said.

"You mean you weren't kissing Alyssa?" Kevin challenged.

"I mean that's only part of the story."

"I don't care about the story," his friend said. "It's Lacey Bolton all over again."

"Seriously, Kev? That was twelve years ago," Jay said. "Can you forget about Lacey Bolton already?"

"Can you not see that this isn't about Lacey Bolton but the guy who screwed over a friend for the sake of a pretty girl?"

"The situation is completely different."

"Not from my perspective," Kevin argued. "You put the moves on a girl you knew I've had my eye on for weeks."

"First, I didn't put any moves on her—*she* kissed *me*," Jay pointed out in his defense. "Second, how is it my fault that you don't have the guts to make a move on a girl you've supposedly had your eye on for weeks?"

"I was waiting for the right moment," Kevin said.

"How long were you going to wait?" Jay wondered.

"Until last night," his friend said. "If you remember, it

was my idea to go to Diggers' last night because I knew Alyssa would be working."

"And if you remember, you left the bar without making any kind of move."

"She was busy," Kevin said in his defense.

"That didn't stop Carter from flirting with her."

Kevin glared at their other friend.

"But all I did was flirt—Jay's the one who kissed her," Carter said, eager to throw Jay under the bus.

He could argue again that she'd kissed *him*, but he couldn't deny that there had been kissing. Instead, he said, "Do you want me to apologize?"

"Are you sorry?" Kevin asked.

He thought about the very public and very brief kiss he'd shared with Alyssa and felt desire stir low in his belly. He could tell Kevin that it wasn't quite as steamy as people were saying, but the memory of that innocent kiss had kept him awake half the night. He could lie, but they'd been friends for too long for that option to sit comfortably with him. "No," he admitted.

Kevin shook his head. "You haven't changed at all."

"What's that supposed to mean?"

"It's always been about the score with you. Jay always has to be with the hottest girls, the most girls—even the unavailable girls."

"I was a dick in high school," he acknowledged. "But we're not in high school anymore."

"You don't think kissing Alyssa was a dick move?"

Of course it was, if he'd done it for the purpose of getting between his friend and the girl he liked. But he hadn't. Nor could he deny that his friend's secret crush on the bartender had been the furthest thing from his mind when Alyssa's mouth touched his.

"Okay, it was," he agreed. "But when you were talking

about the new bartender at Diggers', I had no idea it was Alyssa. If I'd known, I would have told you—weeks ago—that I knew her."

"I don't care that you knew her first—you shouldn't have kissed her."

"I get that this is a guy thing," Nat interjected. "You want to beat your chests to figure out who gets the hot girl, but you're overlooking two key pieces of the puzzle."

"What pieces?" Carter asked.

"First, dibs and friendships aside, it's not up to you to decide who gets Alyssa—it's up to her. And truthfully, I don't know why she'd waste her time with either one of you."

"Thanks," Jay said. "That's very helpful."

"Second," she continued, as if he hadn't spoken, "and this point is really for Kevin…I know you think Jay only kissed Alyssa because he knew you had a crush on her, but that's not true."

"How do you know it's not true?" Kevin demanded.

"Because Jay isn't a big fan of early mornings, but he's been the first one here almost every day for the past several weeks."

"He owns seventy percent of the business—he should be the first one here every day," Kevin pointed out.

"I didn't know there was a gold star for being an early riser," Jay said, giving Nat a subtle shake of his head.

Which she, of course, ignored. "You don't get out of bed early for a gold star—you get out of bed early to go running with Alyssa every morning."

"Is that true?" Kevin asked.

"Every morning, Monday through Friday, since early March," Nat informed them.

And Jay silently cursed himself for ever confiding in her about his new routine with his neighbor.

"That's almost two months," Carter said, obviously surprised by this revelation. "And probably the longest relationship you've had with a woman in years."

"So why haven't you asked her out?" Kevin wondered. "Or did you ask and she shot you down?"

"I didn't ask," Jay said. "Because getting involved with Alyssa would violate the proximity rule."

"Getting involved with anyone in this town would violate the proximity rule," Nat remarked.

"You won't ask her out, but you kissed her last night?"

Jay gave up trying to explain. "It didn't mean anything to either of us."

"Or did it?" Nat conjectured.

"You can butt out anytime now," Jay told her.

"Actually, I want to know what Nat's thinking," Kevin said.

"Tread carefully—a woman's mind can be a complicated and dangerous thing," Carter warned.

Nat glanced at him over her shoulder. "*You* can butt out."

Carter mimed zipping his lips.

"Maybe the kiss didn't mean anything to Jay," Nat allowed. "In which case you're completely justified in being pissed at him. But I think you should give him the benefit of the doubt—and the chance to prove that he didn't kiss her to undermine you, but because he really likes this girl."

"How's he going to prove that?" Kevin challenged.

She considered for a minute. "Jay does seem to have a short attention span when it comes to the women he dates, and the two-month mark is usually when he starts to feel suffocated and look for an escape hatch."

"That's not true," Jay denied.

"Name the last girl you were with for more than two months," she suggested.

He couldn't do it—not without admitting that it had been back when he was in college, and then opening himself up to further analysis of his dating patterns and commitment issues. Maybe being cruelly jilted by his high school girlfriend at a vulnerable time had done a number on him, but he hadn't completely closed off his heart—he just hadn't met a woman whom he wanted to let in.

And while Nat clearly wanted to believe that Alyssa Cabrera might be that woman, Jay remained skeptical.

She turned her attention back to Kevin. "So if Jay invites Alyssa to be his date for Matt's wedding—"

"That's not going to happen," he interjected.

"—then he'd have to be with her for another two months, which might make him crazy—and provide some satisfaction for you."

"What if it doesn't make him crazy?" Kevin challenged.

"Then it would mean he really does have feelings for her," Nat reasoned. "And you wouldn't want to stand in the way of that, would you?"

"I don't know—I'll have to think on that," Kevin told her.

"All of this speculation is moot," Jay said. "Because I'm not asking Alyssa to be my date for Matt's wedding."

"Then I guess our friendship means even less to you than the kiss you shared with her last night."

"Come on, Kev. You know that's not true."

"I'll know it when you invite Alyssa to the wedding."

"Seriously? If I invite Alyssa to the wedding, you'll forgive me for kissing her?"

"She has to accept the invitation," Nat said. "And you can't date any other women between now and then."

Kevin nodded his agreement of the terms.

Jay shook his head, even as he recognized that he'd been neatly backed into a corner. "Okay. I'll do it," he finally relented. Because he and Kevin had been friends for a long time, and because he didn't think dancing with Alyssa at Matt's wedding would be much of a hardship. "Now if we can focus on the business of business, there's a group of fifteen coming in at ten for paintball who will need protective gear, weapons and ammunition."

Carter took the hint—and another doughnut from the box—and headed down to the pro shop.

"Hayley's going to be here around lunchtime to supervise the party room today, but we've got balloons and a cake coming before then," Jay said to Kevin. "Can you keep an eye out for that while you're covering mini putt and the arcade?"

The other man nodded and headed out, leaving Jay and Nat alone—a situation from which she seemed eager to escape.

"I should check the—"

"What the hell?" he said, cutting her off.

She folded her arms across her chest. "Actually, I think the words you're looking for are *thank* and *you*."

"You expect me to be grateful?"

"Yes, because I gave you the excuse you needed to break your ridiculous proximity rule and go out with the girl who's piqued your interest more than anyone has done in a long time."

"I don't need an excuse—if I wanted to break the rule, I would. The fact that I haven't should tell you that I'm—"

"Afraid?" she suggested.

He frowned. "What am I supposedly afraid of?"

"Having a real adult relationship with someone you might be capable of genuinely caring about."

"You don't even know Alyssa," he pointed out.

"True," she acknowledged. "But I know you."

"I'm *not* going to thank you for this."

"Yes, you will," she said and walked out the door.

* * *

Alyssa awakened the next day feeling out of sorts—and grateful that Jason went into work early on Saturdays, so she didn't have to face him this morning. She didn't even want to get dressed and head out for her run, but she knew she'd feel better once she was moving and her adrenaline was pumping. She tried to clear her mind as her feet pounded the pavement, but she couldn't stop thinking about everything that had happened the night before—but mostly about the kiss she'd shared with Jason.

She'd kissed Liam, too. Well, technically, he'd kissed her. But in each case, her lips had made contact with those of a handsome Haven bachelor. But while kissing Liam had felt as dispassionate as kissing a male relative, kissing Jason had been a very different experience.

The minute their mouths had brushed, she'd felt nothing but heat. It was as if she was dry kindling and his lips were a match, the strike of which started a slow burn deep in her belly that quickly spread through her veins, singeing her nerve endings and melting her bones.

Of course, after Diego left, Jason had acted as if it had never happened. He'd certainly given no indication that the moment they'd shared had made any kind of impression on him.

If only she could say the same. The truth was, she hadn't stopped thinking about the kiss. One kiss that couldn't have lasted more than a few seconds. Half a minute at most. And yet, nearly twelve hours later, her lips still tingled.

She was supposed to be an independent woman happily living her own life. But in that brief moment when she'd been kissing Jason, she hadn't wanted to be on her own.

She'd wanted to kiss him again.

She'd wanted to do more than kiss him.

How much more she hadn't realized until she fell asleep and dreamed about him. Incredibly vivid and erotic dreams.

Desperately, she tried to shove the memories of those dreams aside. Because her mind was so unfocused, she forced herself to alter her route, pushing herself to go a little farther and a little faster. But she couldn't outrun her memories of the seductive feel of his lips moving over hers.

After she'd showered and had breakfast, she sat down to mark lab reports. As usual, there were some kids who understood the purpose of the assignment, carefully followed the requisite steps and meticulously recorded their findings, and others whose reports looked as if they had put words and numbers into a blender and randomly scattered them on the page. Those took a lot more focus—and patience—as she attempted to decipher where she could give marks.

After breaking for lunch, she finished up the lab reports and then had absolutely no idea what to do with the rest of her day.

The knock at the door came when she was cleaning out her cupboards. She wasn't expecting any visitors, but Helen Powell sometimes stopped by just to check in with her, and Alyssa always enjoyed those spontaneous drop-ins.

She opened the door expecting to see her elderly across-the-hall neighbor—and found herself looking at her sexy upstairs neighbor instead. Her heart kicked hard against her ribs.

"Hi, honey bear—I'm home."

Then his gaze skimmed over her, from the messy ponytail on top of her head to the old T-shirt and leggings and rubber gloves on her hands, and his smile faded. "You're not ready."

She brushed an errant strand of hair out of her eyes with the back of her arm, embarrassed to have been caught looking so unkempt by a man who always looked so good. "Ready for what?"

"Our date."

She eyed him warily. "Have you been drinking?"

He shook his head slowly, clearly communicating disappointment. "I can't believe you forgot about our plans."

"We didn't have plans."

"For our three-month anniversary," he prompted.

"Our *what*?" Then she remembered the excuse he'd made to Diego the night before, to explain why she wasn't free to have dinner with the other man. "Well, considering that our romantic relationship is entirely fictitious, I trust you can forgive me for not remembering plans we never actually made."

He glanced at his watch. "I can forgive you—if you can be ready in twenty minutes."

"You're serious," she realized.

"I am," he confirmed.

She narrowed her gaze. "Last night you accused me of making a move on you—"

"I was wrong," he acknowledged.

"—and now you're at my door," she noted. "Why?"

"Because you are, by your own admission, a terrible liar, and I don't want you to have to lie to your mother when she asks what we did to celebrate the occasion."

"She won't ask," Alyssa told him.

"Is that a risk you're willing to take rather than put down your bucket and cloth and come with me?"

"Come with you where?" she asked warily.

He responded with the same words she'd spoken to him the night before: "Just go with it."

## Chapter Six

Jay took her to Adventure Village. It wasn't his usual destination for a first date, but he wanted to show off the business he'd built—and have some fun, too.

"I didn't know there was mini golf here," Alyssa admitted when he handed her a putter and an orange ball.

"We started out with a couple of paintball fields, but we've expanded a lot since then," he said proudly. "Hayley is currently designing a new brochure and working on a marketing plan to showcase our newest offerings."

He gestured to the tee area. "Ladies first."

She set her ball down, then crouched to read the green and assess the break.

"Someone takes her mini golf seriously," he mused.

She sent him a quelling glance. "Quiet in the gallery."

His lips curved, but he dutifully remained silent as she lined up her shot.

Her stroke, relaxed and smooth, had the ball rolling up

and over the first hill, gaining enough speed to climb over the next and then come to a stop less than three inches from the cup. His tee shot went out of bounds, costing him a penalty stroke. She finished the first hole with a birdie, he recorded a double bogey.

And that was pretty much par for the course over the next seventeen holes. He did manage a hole in one on number twelve, while Alyssa aced numbers eight, eleven, twelve and fifteen.

"Well, that was fun," he said when he'd tallied up their scores and returned their putters to the rack.

She laughed. "It really was—or at least more fun than washing my kitchen floor."

"Is that how you usually spend your Saturday nights?" he wondered.

"I don't wash the floor every Saturday night," she said. "Sometimes I do windows."

He chuckled as he slid an arm across her shoulders. "While not quite as exciting as that, we do have an arcade where we could kill some time waiting for our dinner to get here," he said, leading her to another room.

Alyssa immediately zeroed in on the Tetris machine. "Do you ever play?" she asked.

He tapped the leaderboard on the screen, pointing to player name JC12 in the second-place position.

"Who's Ford68?" she queried, noting the name in first place.

"My buddy Carter—the one who was pretending not to hit on you last night." Jay pulled a couple tokens out of his pocket. "Do you want to give it a go?"

"Sure," she agreed.

He slid the tokens into the slot, hit the button to select "2-player game" and stood there, watching with his jaw on the ground, as Alyssa effortlessly decimated level after level of the game.

She was still playing when he went to the main entrance to collect and pay for the pizza he'd ordered.

"Are your hands cramping yet?" he asked when he returned to the arcade after setting their food in the party room.

"A little."

"You want to take a break and have some pizza before it gets cold?"

"I just need two more minutes to move into first place on the leaderboard," she told him.

It took her less time than that.

Jay owned the top spot on a couple other games, but he'd never been able to bump Carter out of the number one position on Tetris. Alyssa had done so without breaking a sweat. And watching her had left him feeling both awed…and aroused.

She could have racked up an even higher score, but she stepped away from the game and shook out her hands, flexing her fingers to restore blood flow.

"I didn't know what you liked, so I got half with just cheese and half with pepperoni," he said, turning his attention to their dinner.

"I like pizza," she said.

He opened the box and turned it toward her. She opted for pepperoni, carefully lifting a slice and setting it on the paper plate he'd given her.

"Regular cola, diet cola, orange soda or water?"

"Orange," she decided.

He retrieved two cans from the fridge, then took his seat across from her and selected his pizza.

"You must have spent a lot of time hanging out in arcades while you were growing up," he remarked.

Alyssa shook her head as she peeled a slice of pepperoni off her pizza. "I spent a lot of time with the Game Boy my parents bought to eliminate my boredom while I waited around in hospitals and doctors' offices."

He paused with his can of soda halfway to his mouth. "You were sick?"

She chewed the sausage, swallowed. "I was born with an atrial septal defect—more commonly known as a hole in my heart."

"What does that mean?"

"It means, in my case specifically, that there was an abnormal opening in the upper chambers of my heart," she explained. "I had three surgeries in the first five years of my life, after which the doctors determined that I was perfectly healthy and could do any and everything that all the other kids were doing."

"That must have been a relief."

"You'd think so," she agreed. "But my parents didn't believe the doctors, which meant I was subjected to numerous ongoing tests in their efforts to get a lot of second and third opinions." She lifted the slice of pizza from her plate. "And that was a pretty heavy topic for a fake first date, wasn't it?"

"If there's a list of conversational topics assigned to specific date numbers, I've never seen it," he told her.

She smiled. "Well, I apologize for dumping all that medical history on you."

"No apology necessary," he assured her. "Though I think I'm beginning to understand why you moved from Southern California to northern Nevada."

"It was actually my sister's idea," she confided. "Not Nevada specifically, but the moving away from home."

"Older or younger sister?"

"Older by three years. Cristina's an executive at Google,

married for seven years to a terrific guy with whom she has an adorable almost-five-year-old son."

"Any other siblings?"

She shook her head. "My parents always imagined they'd have a houseful of kids, but that plan was put aside while they focused on making sure I got healthy."

"I've got a brother and two sisters," he said, shifting the focus of the conversation in an attempt to lighten the mood. "All younger. All a pain in my butt while we were growing up. Actually, they're still a pain in my butt most of the time."

She nibbled on her pizza. "Tell me about them."

"My sister Regan is twenty-seven and an accountant at Blake Mining. Spencer is twenty-five and travels the rodeo circuit as a professional cowboy, and Brielle is almost twenty-four and a kindergarten teacher at a private school in Brooklyn."

"That's a long way from home," Alyssa mused.

"She went to New York City to go to college and decided to stay."

"Do you ever visit her there?"

He nodded. "I've been a few times."

"Is it as fabulous as it looks in the movies?" she asked.

"If towering skyscrapers, bumper-to-bumper traffic and oppressive crowds of people are your idea of fabulous."

She smiled, undaunted by his description. "It's been a long-time dream of mine to visit there someday," she admitted. "To see Times Square and Central Park and the Statue of Liberty. To look out over the city from the top of the Empire State Building, see a Broadway show, take in the exhibits at MOMA and the Guggenheim."

"It sounds as if you've given this some thought," he noted.

"A little," she admitted, then laughed. "Or a lot."

"So why haven't you gone?"

It was a good question.

She'd held herself back from doing so many things because she didn't want to give her parents any more cause for concern. And the idea of her youngest daughter traipsing around the country would likely give Renata Cabrera a heart attack.

"Maybe I will," she said. "Someday."

As if on cue, her cell phone rang.

"I have no idea how she does that," Alyssa muttered.

"Who?" Jason asked.

"My mother." She retrieved her phone from the side pocket of her handbag and showed him the display: Mom calling.

"Are you going to answer?"

"I'd rather not," she admitted. "But if I don't, she'll worry that something happened to me, then she'll call again and again until I do."

"Go ahead," he urged. "I'll just sit here and pretend I'm not listening to your conversation."

She was smiling as she connected the call.

But contrary to his admitted intention to eavesdrop, he pushed away from the table and moved to the other side of the room to put the leftover pizza in the fridge.

Alyssa didn't talk to her mother for very long, and when she tucked the phone away again, she asked him, "What did you say to Diego last night?"

Though she'd attempted to keep her tone neutral, some of the tension she felt must have been reflected in the question, because he responded cautiously.

"I get the feeling that you're looking for something specific, but I honestly don't remember all the details of our conversation."

"Did you tell him that I was the woman you'd dreamed

about long before we ever met, and that you couldn't wait for me to meet your family?"

"That does sound vaguely familiar," he confirmed. "An inspired off-the-cuff performance, if I do say so myself."

"You could have talked about anything else," she pointed out to him. "The Golden Knights' inaugural season, or the expansion of the subdivision on the west side of town, or even the price of tea in China. Why did you have to make up details about our nonexistent relationship?"

"Because Diego wasn't interested in any topic of conversation that wasn't you," he told her.

She shook her head. "I only meant for you to play along *in the moment*, but you took over directing and rewrote the whole script."

"What's the big deal?" he asked, unconcerned.

"The big deal is that my parents are now coming to Haven to meet you."

"Whoa!" Jay held up his hands and took an instinctive step backward, as if that might distance him from the very possibility. "I don't do meeting the parents."

"Believe me, I want them to meet you even less than you want to meet them," Alyssa said grimly.

He should be relieved she was letting him off the hook, but he couldn't help but feel a little insulted by her response. "Why don't you want them to meet me?"

"Because you're not actually my boyfriend," she reminded him.

"Okay, that's a valid point," he acknowledged.

"And now I'm going to have to tell my mother that we broke up and she'll tell Diego, and the next time I see him, he'll want to help me mend my broken heart."

"You don't look particularly brokenhearted to me," he remarked.

She dropped her face in her hands. "How did this happen to me?"

Again, he knew she wasn't really expecting an answer, but he couldn't resist teasing, "Because you lied to your mother."

"You're joking," she noted. "But maybe it's true."

"Are you suggesting that the earth's rotation is dependent on some kind of maternal karma?"

"Of course not. But there's no denying a mother's intuition," she told him.

He thought of his own mother and wasn't convinced. Margaret Blake-Channing had been too involved in her career to know—or even care—what her kids were up to most of the time. In fact, he had trouble believing that she'd been away from her office long enough to conceive and bear four children. Of course, considering that both his parents worked at Blake Mining, it was possible she hadn't left her desk at all—and that was not something he wanted to be thinking about right now. Or ever.

Not that he had any cause for complaint. He'd grown up with a lot of privileges and, though his parents had both worked long hours, Celeste had been there to ensure homework was supervised and proper meals put on the table. But the nanny/housekeeper wasn't a strict disciplinarian, so Jay had never felt the need to lie to her.

"Why do you say that?" he asked Alyssa now.

"Because anytime I've been less than completely honest with her, she's somehow known it."

"Maybe you're just a bad liar," he suggested.

"I am a bad liar," she agreed. "I don't like lying—especially to my parents. And every time I'm even just a little bit untruthful, my mother somehow knows it."

"Give me an example," he urged.

"In my junior year of high school, I was out with my

friends and took a few puffs of a cigarette that was offered to me. As soon as I got home, she asked if I'd
been smoking—which, of course, I denied—and then
she grounded me for smoking *and* lying."

"She probably smelled smoke on your clothes," he
pointed out logically.

"And when my friend Karen swiped a bottle of vodka
from her parents' liquor cabinet and we mixed it in our
lemonade at the Fourth of July picnic, she asked if I'd been
drinking. And there was no way she could smell that because it was vodka."

"How old were you?"

"Seventeen," she admitted.

"So maybe there were other signs that you'd been con-
suming alcohol," he suggested drily.

"Maybe," she acknowledged.

"So your mother caught you in lies about smoking and
drinking, and you think that proves she has some kind of
sixth sense about when you're lying?"

"And then there was the time I asked to go to a movie
with my best friend—and I didn't tell her that we were
meeting a couple of boys there, too. But somehow she
knew."

"Isn't it possible that someone saw you at the theater
with the boys and told her?"

"Of course," she agreed. "But the point is that she always knows when I'm not telling her the truth."

"So that's it? You've lied to her a total of three times
in your life?"

"Four, including the boyfriend thing," she said. "Big
lies, that is. There have been smaller ones that she lets me
get away with—such as when I tell her that the chicken
isn't too dry, or I like her new haircut."

"And maybe she doesn't have a clue that you're being

less than truthful about the boyfriend, and she sincerely wants to meet the guy you've been dating."

"This is all Liam's fault," Alyssa decided. "If he had been there when he said he was going to be, I would have kissed him instead of you."

"So are you and Gilmore…a thing?"

"No," she said. "I told you—I'm not dating anyone and I don't *want* to date anyone."

"Why not?" he asked curiously.

"Because I'm enjoying living my own life."

"Why would dating someone change that?"

"It wouldn't, necessarily, if it was someone other than Diego," she acknowledged. "But if I consented to a friendly dinner with my mother's best friend's favorite nephew, that friendly dinner would lead to casual dating, which would then transition into an exclusive relationship and a ring on my finger."

"You really believe that, don't you?"

She shook her head. "That's why, when my mother called to tell me that Diego was going to be in Haven, I came up with the phony boyfriend plan. But Liam wasn't there and I kissed you, and you had coffee with Diego and now…" She sighed. "It's been nice fake dating you, but now I have to figure out how to explain our breakup to my parents."

"Here's a novel idea," he said. "Why don't you tell them the truth—that you're not dating anyone because you don't want to date anyone?"

She chewed on her bottom lip as she considered her options. "Maybe I could still make this work with Liam." The furrow in her brow deepened. "Obviously I'll have to find out what other details from your conversation Diego passed along to my mother."

"Such as your boyfriend's name?" he suggested.

She closed her eyes and wearily said, "Yeah, that could put a wrench in things."

"You think?"

"Unless—" her eyes popped open again "—I can get Liam to pretend that he's you, just for one night."

"That's not gonna happen, either," he told her.

"How do you know?"

"Because he's a Gilmore."

"And?" she prompted.

"And although my last name is Channing, my mother was a Blake."

"How is that relevant?" she asked.

"You haven't heard about the Blake-Gilmore feud," he realized.

"Nothing more than a vague comment from Sky last night," she admitted.

"It's a long story," he said, "but the gist of it is that the Blakes and the Gilmores came to Nevada to settle the same piece of land more than a hundred and fifty years ago. Rather than admit they'd both been duped, they agreed to split the property."

"So what's the problem?"

"Everett Gilmore arrived first and, having already started to build his homestead, took the prime grazing land for his cattle, leaving Samuel Blake with the less hospitable terrain. As a result, the Crooked Creek Ranch—and the family—struggled for a lot of years until gold and silver were discovered in their hills."

"And now both families are rich," she noted.

"But the animosity persists," he told her.

She sighed. "I know I have no right to ask you for any favors, but if you could just meet my parents—"

Jay was shaking his head before she finished talking. "No."

"It doesn't have to be a big deal," she promised. "Just a quick get-together, maybe throw in a mention about how nice it is to finally meet the parents you've heard so much about and—"

"I've heard nothing about them. I don't even know their names."

"Miguel and Renata," she supplied helpfully.

"Which doesn't change anything," he said. "I don't ever meet the parents of a girl I'm actually dating, so to meet the parents of a girl I've never even kissed…" He shook his head. "Not going to happen."

"Except that you did kiss me," she pointed out.

"No," he argued. "*You* kissed *me*."

Her brow furrowed as she considered the distinction. "How does that make any difference?"

"Honey, if I'd made a move on you, I guarantee it wouldn't have been in a crowded bar on a Friday night with a counter between us."

And even while he was trying to remember all the reasons he wasn't willing to make that move, he found his gaze drawn to the delicate shape and tempting fullness of her lips. The brief kiss she'd planted on him less than twenty-four hours earlier had made more of an impression than he wanted to admit, and stirred desires he couldn't let himself acknowledge.

"Okay, then," she finally relented.

But he could tell that she was still trying to come up with an alternate plan.

"Tell them the truth," he suggested again.

"The truth will lead to me walking down the aisle in a white dress before the end of next summer."

"I'm sure you're exaggerating."

"If you'd agree to maintain this charade long enough to meet my parents, you'd realize I'm not."

"Yeah, that's not gonna happen." But even as he said the words, he remembered the promise he'd made to Kevin and silently cursed his predicament.

He'd planned this outing as a way of breaking the ice with Alyssa, showing her that he was interesting and fun so that she'd agree to go to Matt's wedding with him. It was the price Kevin had demanded for his forgiveness, but the instinctive panic that flooded Jay's mind at the prospect of "meeting the parents" had momentarily pushed everything else aside.

Now that the panic had begun to recede, he was beginning to see that her dilemma could lead to a win for both of them.

"I need to learn to stand up to my parents—I know I do," she admitted. "But as nosy and interfering as they can be, I know it's only because they worry about me."

"How old are you?" he asked curiously.

"Twenty-six."

"Isn't that old enough to be living on your own?"

"Of course it is," she agreed. "But they've always been a little…overprotective."

"Because of the heart thing?" he guessed.

She nodded.

"I don't mean to sound unsympathetic," he said. "But the overprotectiveness is their problem, not yours."

"I know," she agreed, pushing away from the table. "Thank you for an enjoyable evening, but I'd like to go home now and try to figure out plan C."

"Does plan C involve Gilmore?"

"I don't know yet."

"Then let's talk about plans for tomorrow before you do anything too hasty," he suggested.

She frowned. "What plans for tomorrow?"

"I'm free for dinner. And that chili you made the day of the storm was really good."

"You want me to cook dinner for you?"

"I'm going to be working all day," he pointed out as he rose to his feet. "And it sure would be nice to come home and share a meal with my doting girlfriend."

"You've already made it clear that you don't want any part of this."

"Maybe our conversation over dinner will change my mind."

Her gaze narrowed. "You're totally playing me, aren't you?"

"There's only one way to find out, isn't there?"

She forced a smile. "Dinner's at six."

## Chapter Seven

Alyssa knew Jason's suggestion that she might change his mind about meeting her parents was simply a ploy for a home-cooked meal. Well, she was ninety-nine percent certain of it.

But if there was even a one percent chance that she might be able to change his mind, she had to take it.

And even if he was playing her for a free dinner, she figured she owed him that much for not exposing her deception to Diego. Plus, she liked to cook, and cooking for Jason gave her an excuse to prepare something she wouldn't generally make for herself.

Of course, that meant a trip to The Trading Post, Haven's all-purpose general/grocery/liquor store. Lizzie Cartwright was working the cash register and, as she scanned the items, immediately wanted to know who Alyssa was cooking the special meal for. She tried to convince the woman that she was just experimenting with a new recipe, but as she paid for her groceries, she could tell that Lizzie didn't believe her.

Still, she'd prefer to be the subject of speculation rather than gossip, and if she told anyone that she was cooking for her upstairs neighbor, the rumor mill would be churning before she got home and got her groceries unpacked. Of course, if she'd been thinking clearly, she would have gone to Battle Mountain to shop and avoided exactly this scenario. But she hadn't been thinking straight since she'd kissed Jason.

Which was another reason she should abandon her plan—or at least her efforts to enlist his help. Because spending time with him and pretending to be infatuated with him could lead to a real infatuation.

She covered the skillet and set it in the oven to keep the chicken warm, checked the potatoes and added the washed and trimmed asparagus spears to the tray. She minced some fresh garlic and warmed it in a small pan with olive oil, then poured the warm oil into a shallow bowl, added oregano, black pepper, balsamic vinegar and fresh Parmesan.

When everything was ready, she touched up her makeup. Just a quick brush of powder to eliminate the shine from working over the stove, a touch of mascara to her lashes and a dab of gloss on her lips. And then she changed her clothes, too.

She hadn't planned to dress up. Just because she'd been manipulated into making dinner didn't make this a date. On the other hand, jeans with frayed cuffs and an old T-shirt were perhaps a little too casual if she expected him to give any consideration to her potential as a girlfriend—even a temporary one. So she pulled on a tunic-style blouse over a long skirt, added a metal chain-link belt and a pair of chunky heels and tried to ignore the butterflies fluttering in her tummy, because this wasn't a big deal. This was just a woman sharing a meal with a man she saw almost every day.

But planning the menu, shopping for groceries and preparing the food somehow made the simple act of sharing a meal feel more like a date.

Except that she didn't date guys like Jason.

He was too good-looking, too charismatic, too self-assured. And definitely too egotistical. She couldn't believe his suggestion that she'd made up the phony boyfriend story as an excuse to kiss him! She was still appalled by the idea.

On the other hand, if even half the rumors around town were to be believed, some women had gone to extreme lengths to get close to one of Haven's most sought-after bachelors. And sought-after bachelors like Jason definitely didn't date girls like her.

So she needed to relax and remember that this was just a friendly meal over which she would make a half-hearted attempt to convince him to go along with her fake dating plan, and he would, ultimately, refuse. At the end of the evening, he would thank her for the meal and say goodnight, then go back to his own apartment without a kiss.

Yes, it would definitely be smart to end the evening without a kiss.

But it wasn't what she wanted…

It was more of a negotiation than a date, but Jay found himself stopping at The Trading Post to pick up a bottle of wine and a six-pack of his favorite beer anyway. Then he made a second stop at Garden of Eden, the local flower shop, where he took too long surveying the array of options before finally selecting a mixed bouquet of mostly orange and yellow blooms.

When he finally got home, he showered quickly, then

realized he'd forgotten to shave before heading to work that morning. He took an extra few minutes to raze the stubble from his jaw and knocked at Alyssa's door at 6:02 p.m.

He exhaled an audible sigh of relief when she answered the door. "Good—you're still here."

She frowned in response to the unorthodox greeting. "Where else would I be?"

"I don't know," he admitted. "But the one morning I was two minutes late for our run, you were at the end of the street before I caught up with you."

"That's because starting out late on *my* run would have thrown off my entire schedule for the day," she pointed out.

He offered her the flowers.

"Oh." She looked at the blossoms wrapped in decorative paper as if she wasn't entirely sure what to do with them.

"Now you say 'thank you' and put them in some water," he suggested.

"Thank you," she said, accepting the bouquet.

"You're welcome."

She stepped away from the door so he could enter.

He followed her to the kitchen, where she bent to look in the cupboard under the sink, emerging with a glass vase that she tipped under the faucet to fill with water.

"This is for you, too." He handed her the bottle of wine when she finished with the flowers.

"You're observant," she commented, noting that the label matched the one on the bottle they'd been drinking the other night.

"I brought beer, too," he said, holding up the six-pack in his other hand.

She took the beer from him and put it in the fridge. "Thirsty?" she guessed.

He grinned. "And hungry. I skipped lunch."

"There's bread warming in the oven and dip on the table."

"Bread and dip?" he echoed dubiously. "That's what's for dinner?"

She chuckled softly. "No, it's an appetizer."

"So what's for dinner?" he asked.

"Chicken marsala with oven-roasted vegetables."

"I guess you know how to make more than chili," he noted.

"I do," she confirmed. "And I like to cook."

"So…if you were dating someone, how often would you cook for him?"

"I don't know." She pulled a tray of bread from the oven, then began transferring the slices to a basket. "It would probably depend on how often he takes me out to eat."

"You're supposed to be convincing me to go along with your boyfriend plan," he reminded her.

She waved a hand dismissively. "That was last night. Today, I've accepted that you're unwilling to be convinced."

"But you made dinner for me anyway?"

"I like to cook," she said again. "Plus, you fed me last night, so it seemed like a fair trade."

She gestured for him to sit, then set the basket of warm bread on the table.

"Do you want a glass of wine or a beer?"

"I'll have a beer—if it won't be an insult to your chicken."

She popped the top on one of the bottles, poured it into a glass and set it on the table already set for two with fancy dishes, gleaming cutlery and linen napkins.

"When I finagled a dinner invitation, I really didn't expect you to go to so much trouble," he told her.

"It wasn't any trouble. I love these dishes and I hardly ever get to use them." She peered into the window of the oven door, checking on whatever was inside. "And I should have asked you last night if you have any food allergies."

"No allergies," he told her as he dipped a piece of bread into the shallow bowl of oil and vinegar and spices.

He popped the bread into his mouth, and the flavors exploded on his tongue.

"This is delicious," he said, dipping his bread again.

She took a slice from the basket, tore off a piece and dipped it. She nodded as she chewed. "It is good."

"You haven't made this before?"

"I've made different variations of it," she admitted. "I often tweak recipes I find online to make them my own."

She opened the bottle of wine, poured a glass.

"Aren't you supposed to drink white wine with chicken?"

"Asks the man drinking Icky," she noted.

He lifted his glass. "Beer goes with everything."

"And this pinot noir pairs nicely with the marsala."

He selected another piece of bread from the basket. "What would you have been eating for dinner tonight if you weren't cooking for me?"

"Probably chicken," she said. "But more likely just baked in the oven and served on top of a salad."

He made a face. "Girl food."

"In case you haven't noticed, I *am* a girl."

"I noticed," he assured her, his gaze skimming over her in a leisurely and thorough perusal. "I very definitely noticed."

She chewed on another bite of bread.

He wondered if the flush in her cheeks was from the heat of the stove or the sexual awareness that simmered between them.

"There's a rumor that Adventure Village is adding a go-kart track to its offerings this summer," she said.

"Are you interested in go-karts or just trying to change the subject?"

"Just making conversation." She opened the oven door, then pulled out the tray of vegetables and the pan of chicken.

"Fingers crossed, the track will be ready by the first of June," he said.

"That should keep you busy through the summer."

"It's keeping me busy now," he admitted.

She arranged the food on two plates, carried them to the table. "Then it's probably a good thing that I've decided to recast the pretend boyfriend role."

He surveyed the plate she set in front of him. The chicken and potatoes looked and smelled delicious, but he was wary of the green stuff.

"I'm not a fan of asparagus," he said, poking it with his fork.

"You've never had my asparagus," she pointed out to him. "Try it."

He picked up his fork and knife and sliced into the chicken instead. "And what do you mean—you've decided to recast the role?"

"I've had a lot of time to think about this today," she told him. "And while I understand now why Liam might have some reservations about pretending to be a Blake— or Channing—especially after your snarky comment the other night—"

"What snarky comment was that?"

"—I think," she continued, ignoring his interruption and his question, "with the right incentive, I can get him to go along with my plan."

Jay scowled. "What kind of incentive are you planning to offer?"

"I don't think it would be appropriate to discuss those details with you."

His brows lifted.

Color flooded her cheeks. "Ohmygod—no! Not… No!" she said again. "How could you even think…"

"You can't blame my mind for going there," he said. "You mentioned an incentive, and that would be a definite incentive."

"Uh…thank you?" she said dubiously.

"It was a compliment," he assured her.

"Well, I only intended to offer to help Liam with a… situation," she said, reaching for her wineglass.

"Heather Cross still trying to lure him back?" he guessed.

"What do you know about Liam's relationship with Heather?"

"Haven't you lived here long enough to know that there are no secrets in Haven?" He popped a bite-size potato into his mouth.

"Apparently not."

"Well, believe me, that's a mess you don't want to get in the middle of."

Alyssa sighed. "I'm running out of options."

"There's always the truth."

"You met Diego," she reminded him.

"And the guy is seriously infatuated with you," he acknowledged.

"My mother's fault," she said. "I've done nothing to encourage him, but he refuses to believe that I'm not interested."

"And you figured shoving another guy in his face would do the trick?"

"Desperate times," she said.

His brows lifted. "That's the second time you've said that you kissed me because you were desperate."

"And because Liam wasn't there," she reminded him.

"Now you're shoving another guy in *my* face," he noted.

"Liam's not 'another guy'—he's the one who was expected to be my boyfriend."

"You mean pretend boyfriend."

"No one was supposed to know that part," she reminded him. "And since you've already made it clear that you have no intention of maintaining the charade or meeting my parents, why are we even having this conversation?"

"I'm reconsidering," he told her.

"Why don't I believe you?"

"I don't know. Maybe you're inherently distrustful."

"And maybe you don't seem like the kind of guy who would be swayed by chicken marsala."

"I wouldn't have thought so, either," he acknowledged. "But this chicken is delicious."

"Thank you," she said.

But it wasn't really the chicken that had made him reconsider his position. Aside from wanting to mend fences with his buddy, her willingness—even eagerness—to turn to Liam Gilmore for help was probably the biggest reason he'd decided to help her out.

Maybe it was petty, but it was true. As much as Jay had never wanted the boyfriend role that Alyssa was offering, he was even less inclined to let Liam Gilmore fill it.

"Of course, I would have some conditions if I was to go along with your plan," he said to her now.

"Such as?" she asked warily.

"A home-cooked meal like this twice a week for the duration of our phony relationship."

"You expect me to cook for you on a schedule?"

"I'm horribly incompetent in the kitchen," he confided. "And eating microwaveable meals gets tiresome day after day."

"I'm sure it does," she agreed.

"Even two good meals a week would help break up the monotony," he said, his tone imploring.

"One a week," she countered.

"Two would benefit you as much as me," he told her.

"How do you figure?"

"Because I'd be saving you from a boring menu of grilled chicken and salads."

A smile tugged at her lips, but she came back with another counteroffer. "Three meals over the course of two weeks."

Though they both knew that he was negotiating from a position of power, he admired her refusal to cave to his demands. "That's acceptable," he finally decided.

She offered her hand, as if to seal the bargain, but he shook his head.

"That's only the first condition," he told her.

"What else do you want?" she asked.

"Reciprocity." He picked up the bottle of wine and topped up her glass.

"You want me to meet *your* parents?"

"Ha! No. I want a date for Matt's wedding."

"Who?"

"Matt Hutchinson—one of the guys I was with at Diggers' the other night."

"When's the wedding?"

"July 14."

"That's more than two months away," she pointed out.

"You plan on dumping me before then?"

"I'm thinking it's more likely you'll meet someone else you'd rather take to the wedding before then."

"How and when would I meet someone else when I'm going to be spending all my free time with my adoring girlfriend?"

"I don't do adoring," she warned him. "And my parents wouldn't believe it if I tried."

"Pity," he said. "But the truth is, a wedding can be a tricky event for a single guy. If he shows up alone, most people think he couldn't get a date."

"No one would think you were incapable of getting a date," she assured him.

"A compliment?" he wondered.

"A fact."

"Going solo also makes a man vulnerable to the advances of the single women who desperately don't want to be at a wedding alone."

"I have no doubt you could fend them off, if you really wanted to," she said.

"I'd rather not have to," he said. "And the problem with asking a casual girlfriend to attend a wedding is that she inevitably thinks the invitation means something more than just a date."

"So you're asking for three home-cooked meals over the next two weeks and the option of a date for your friend's wedding in July," she noted. "Anything else you want?"

He thought about her question for a minute, considering various creative demands to add to his list—most that he knew she would refuse. In the end, he only said, "Dessert?"

# Chapter Eight

Alyssa glanced pointedly at his plate. "You haven't eaten your asparagus."

"Green vegetables aren't really my thing," Jay told her.

"Is dessert your thing?" she asked.

His head lifted. "What's for dessert?"

"Strawberry and mascarpone tart."

He looked at his plate again, stabbed one of the spears with the tines of his fork and tentatively nibbled on the end. "This is…not bad," he decided.

"Hardly a rousing endorsement, but I'll take it," she said.

He had another bite. "FYI, for future meals, you can stick to meat and potatoes."

"FYI, in my kitchen, you eat the healthy and balanced meal that's put in front of you or you don't get dessert," she told him.

He finished off the asparagus.

She pushed away from the table to clear his now empty plate along with her own.

"Do you want coffee?" she offered, reaching into the cupboard for dessert plates.

"No, thanks."

But he did want a sneak peek at dessert—and another beer—so he followed her to the refrigerator. "That looks really good," he said as he reached over her shoulder for a bottle.

She bobbled the pan she was sliding off the shelf.

"Easy," he said, catching the bottom of the dish.

"I didn't... I thought—" She glanced at the table, where she'd expected him to still be sitting, then blew out a breath. "Sorry—you startled me."

"I would have been really sorry if you'd dropped that tart," he said.

"I've got it," she assured him.

He took it from her and turned to set it on the counter, but he didn't step away from her. And standing so close, he could see the pulse point at the base of her jaw—and how fast it was beating.

He pushed the door of the fridge closed, forgetting about the beer that had been his reason for getting up in the first place. "I have a confession to make."

"What's that?"

"Even before we sat down to eat, I'd decided to give this fake dating thing a shot."

"Why?"

"Because of the kiss," he admitted.

"The kiss?" she echoed.

"Since that kiss across the bar at Diggers', I've found myself thinking about kissing you again."

"You have?"

He nodded. "It also occurred to me that I've been a

lousy boyfriend if that was our first kiss after three months of dating."

"Except that we haven't actually been dating for three months," she pointed out.

"But if we're going to convince your parents that we've been dating for— Actually, it would be closer to four months by Memorial Day weekend, wouldn't it?"

"I guess it would," Alyssa confirmed, albeit with obvious reluctance.

"Then you're going to have to get used to me kissing you."

"My parents are only going to be here for a weekend," she reminded him. "I'm sure we can manage to keep our hands off one another for that brief period of time."

"What if I don't want to keep my hands off you?" he asked, setting those hands on her hips.

"I thought you wanted dessert," she said.

He could see the nervousness in her eyes, but there was attraction there, too. She might deny that she wanted him to kiss her, but they both knew that she did.

"I do," he said and lowered his mouth to hers.

It was true that he'd been thinking about kissing her again, but he hadn't intended to make a move this soon.

Sure, her dating charade would necessitate sharing some touches and kisses, and he certainly had no objection to getting up close and personal with his sexy neighbor. But he'd expected to be able to exercise some restraint. He hadn't anticipated that being close to her would stir him up so much that he didn't just want to kiss her—he *needed* to kiss her.

He needed to know if her mouth was as soft and sweet as he remembered. The barest touch of his lips to hers confirmed his recollection—and made him want more.

Desire, sharp and needy, clawed at his belly, urging him to take everything she offered.

Her hands slid up his chest to hook over his shoulders, holding on as he continued to kiss her. Her lips parted beneath the pressure of his; her tongue danced with his, following his lead.

Their first kiss had been a teasing and tentative exploration. This kiss, from the first touch of their mouths, was different. More urgent. More intense. And much hotter.

His hand slid around her waist, over her bottom, pulling her closer. She gasped as the evidence of his arousal pressed against her belly, but she didn't pull away. In fact, she pushed her hips against him, making him burn with a desire that he held firmly—and painfully—in check.

When he'd lowered his mouth to hers, he'd been certain that he was in control of the situation. But the press of her soft body against him made him realize how slippery his grasp was on that control. And the soft, sexy sounds that emanated from her throat threatened to break even that tenuous grip.

With sincere regret, he loosened his hold on her and took a careful step back.

Alyssa blinked up at him—confusion and arousal churning in her veins. She drew in a slow, deep breath and willed her rubbery legs to help her remain standing.

"Do you want to talk about it?" Jason asked, after several seconds had passed during which the silence was broken only by the sounds of their ragged breathing.

She didn't need to ask what "it" was. Not while the heat of the kiss they'd shared continued to simmer in the air between them.

"No." She turned away to reach into the drawer for the pastry cutter, tightening her grip on the handle when she realized her hands were trembling. Truthfully, her whole body was trembling, but she had no intention of letting him know it. She sliced into the tart. "Except to say that you can't kiss me like that anymore."

"How do you want me to kiss you?"

She didn't have to look at him to see the smile tugging at the corners of his mouth—she could hear the amusement in his tone. "I don't want you to kiss me at all," she said as she transferred the slice of tart to a plate.

"Liar."

She huffed out a breath. "I'm not denying that there's a certain…attraction," she decided. "But I'm not going to sleep with you."

"I'm not asking you to sleep with me," he told her.

"Well, that's good, then," she said, torn between relief and disappointment as she added a dessert fork to his plate.

"Not because I don't think we could have a lot of fun naked and horizontal together," he clarified. "But because, under the circumstances, having sex would only complicate the situation."

"The last thing I want right now is another complication," she assured him.

He nodded. "There is one more thing we need to be clear about."

"What's that?"

"This phony relationship isn't ever going to lead to anything more, because I don't do relationships."

"I don't want anything more," she promised him.

Because that had been the absolute truth in the beginning. All she'd wanted was a pretend boyfriend to convince her mother that she was settled and happy in Haven—so that Renata would stop trying to set her up with other guys.

But now that she'd spent more time with Jason—now that he'd kissed her senseless—she found her heart yearning for more.

\* \* \*

Alyssa Skyped with Nicolas on his birthday, enjoying a fun—and long—conversation with her now five-year-old nephew, who insisted that she watch while he assembled the Lego set she'd sent to him. His little brow furrowed with concentration as he worked, and she was grateful for the technology that allowed her not just to talk to him but actually see him. It wasn't quite the same as being there, and she missed the feeling of his slender arms around her and the baby shampoo scent of his hair, but the visual connection helped.

She was looking forward to talking to her sister, too. She could always count on Cristina to listen to her woes and offer insightful advice. Not that spending time with Jason Channing was a cause for distress by any stretch of the imagination, but she needed someone to tell her that she hadn't made a huge mistake in the bargain they'd struck.

Except that when Cristina took the iPad from her son, Alyssa was greeted by a barrage of questions about her new boyfriend—because, of course, Renata had already shared the news. In fact, Alyssa wouldn't be surprised to learn that her mother had ended the call with her and immediately dialed her other daughter's number.

"This is the hunky guy who's been your running partner over the past few months, right?" Cristina asked, then forged ahead without waiting for a response. "I so hoped something would click between the two of you."

"You did?" Alyssa asked, surprised. "Why?"

"Because it was obvious from your very first mention that you were attracted to him."

"It was?"

"And shared hobbies and interests always help build a stronger relationship."

"Well, I wouldn't exactly call what we have a relationship," Alyssa hedged. "In fact—"

"I know you're a little wary," Cristina interjected. "And I understand why. But it's past time for you to open up and let somebody love you the way you deserve to be loved."

"But—"

"I know the relationship is fairly new and you probably think I'm jumping the gun, and maybe I am a little," her sister acknowledged. "But I want you to be happy. And, of course, a woman doesn't need a man to be happy, but sharing your life with someone really does have its rewards. And it's such a relief to know that I can stop worrying about you now."

That gave Alyssa pause.

She knew that her parents worried, which was why she tried to spare them the details of her darkest thoughts and deepest concerns. But she'd never held back with Cristina, and she hadn't realized that sharing her doubts and insecurities had caused her sister to worry about her, too.

So when Cristina stopped talking long enough to take a breath and Alyssa finally had the chance to tell her that the relationship with Jason was a charade, she couldn't do it. Instead, she only said, "Now tell me what's new with you."

And for the next half hour, they talked about other things while Alyssa felt the tangled web drawing tighter around her.

Jay was shutting down his computer late the following Saturday afternoon when Hayley poked her head into the room. Kevin had taken the day off to help a friend move, Nat and Carter were throwing darts in the office-slash-lounge and Matt was texting on his phone.

"After back-to-back preteen birthday parties, I could really use some adult company tonight," she said.

"There's a new Daniel Craig movie playing at the local theater," Carter said.

Hayley nodded. "That sounds good to me."

"I'm in," Nat agreed. "But I want food first."

"Matt?" Carter prompted.

The other man shook his head. "I promised to help Carrie work on the seating plan tonight."

"Has she turned into Bridezilla yet?" Hayley asked.

"Of course not," Matt denied. "Though she did ask me to prompt you for the name of your guest for the place card."

"You know my guest," she said. "I told you that Carter and I are going together."

"But you responded with plus-guest on the reply card," Matt reminded her.

"Well, yeah, 'cause I'm not showing up to your wedding without a date."

The groom-to-be looked at Carter. "You responded with plus-guest, too."

"Because I'm going with Hayley," he said.

Matt shook his head. "Carrie was worried about how we were going to split you guys up—because the tables only seat eight, and if you all brought dates, you couldn't be seated at the same table."

"Well, now that problem's solved, isn't it?" Hayley said helpfully.

"Except that Matt and Carrie probably ordered two extra meals for guests who aren't going to be there," Nat—who'd spent six months planning her own wedding for a marriage that didn't last half that long—pointed out to her friends.

"Oh." Hayley looked at Matt, obviously chagrined. "I didn't think about that."

"It's fine," he said.

"Kevin have a date for the big day?" Jay asked.

Matt nodded. "He's bringing Sydney, the girl he's helping move today."

"But don't think that means he's forgiven you for the whole Alyssa thing," Nat warned him.

"There was no 'Alyssa thing' except in his mind," Jay said.

"Note to self—do not seat Kevin beside hot bartender," Matt said, moving toward the door.

"Kevin would probably worry more about Jay being seated near Sydney, in case he decides to steal another girl he's got his eye on."

"I didn't steal Alyssa," Jay said, just a little defensively.

"She's your date for the wedding, isn't she?" Hayley pressed.

"Only because Nat forced my hand." Which was true, and yet not nearly the whole truth.

"And all this time you've been spending with her in the interim—that must be a real hardship, huh?" Carter said.

Of course, it hadn't been a hardship but a pleasure. He sincerely enjoyed hanging out with Alyssa and was grateful that their charade gave him a ready excuse to do so.

"Can we forget about Jay's love life and focus on our plans for tonight?" Nat suggested. "Preferably the food part."

"I'm sick of pizza," Carter said.

"Diggers' it is, then," Hayley decided.

"You in, Jay?" Nat asked.

He shook his head. "Alyssa's making dinner for me tonight."

"This is getting to be a regular thing," Hayley noted.

He shrugged. "She likes to cook."

Nat smirked. "Is that what the kids are calling it these days?"

He shook his head. "Get your head out of the gutter."

"You're not sleeping with her?" she challenged.

"Of course I'm not sleeping with her."

"Why is that an 'of course'?" Carter wondered.

"Because we're only pretend dating."

Nat frowned. "What do you mean?"

"Thanks to your interference, I had to ask Alyssa to be my date for Matt's wedding, in exchange for which I agreed to be her pretend boyfriend when her parents come to town."

Hayley smirked. "You had to bribe a girl to go out with you?"

"We entered into a mutually beneficial agreement."

"I don't think this is what Kevin had in mind," Nat said.

"You mean it's not what *you* had in mind."

She didn't dispute the point.

"Obviously I missed something," Hayley said.

"That's right—you weren't here last week for the big confrontation after Jay kissed the girl Kevin had his eye on and Nat had to play peacemaker."

"Peacemaker or matchmaker?" Jay wondered.

"And now you're going to meet her parents?" Hayley pressed.

"It's not a big deal. Her mom and dad are going to be in town for the long weekend, so I'll spend some time with them, play the boyfriend role, then they'll go back to California and the status quo will be restored."

"And you and Alyssa will just be friends and neighbors again?" Nat asked skeptically.

"Why not?"

She shrugged. "What if all this pretending leads to the development of real feelings?"

"That's not going to happen," he said confidently.

"Maybe not for you," Carter acknowledged. "But what about Alyssa?"

"No worries there," he assured him. "She isn't interested in a real relationship right now."

"I still think you're playing a dangerous game," Hayley warned. "Then again—games are what you do best, aren't they?"

Alyssa seasoned the pork roast with garlic, rosemary and thyme and served it with wild rice and green beans with dried cranberries. She'd considered doing carrots instead of the beans but couldn't resist the challenge of putting a green vegetable on Jason's plate again.

While they ate, he talked about his plans for the grand opening of the go-kart track and his intention to do a test run before the end of the following week. In fact, he was so caught up in his excitement over this prospect, he ate the beans without protest.

After dinner, Alyssa carried the platter of meat and vegetables to the counter to wrap up the leftovers. Jason followed with their plates and cutlery and began loading the dishwasher.

"You don't have to do that," she protested, as she did after every meal they shared. And every time, he insisted on doing kitchen duty.

"It's the least I can do to show my appreciation."

"You're going to be paying with fake love and phony devotion," she reminded him.

"A hefty price," he agreed. "Maybe I should have held out for a couple extra meals."

"Too late now—the bargain's been struck."

He moved away from the dishwasher and opened the fridge, scanning the contents. "Where's dessert?"

"What dessert?"

"You really didn't make anything for dessert?"

He looked so sincerely disappointed, she almost felt guilty for teasing him. "Of course I did," she said. "It's in the oven."

He immediately reached for the handle of the oven.

"Don't." She shoved him back and slapped her hand against the door before he could pull it open. "Letting the heat out will affect the baking time."

He dutifully tucked his hands behind him. "The baking time of what?"

"Chocolate lava cake."

His eyes lit up. "When will it be ready?"

"When the timer goes off."

He glanced at the numbers ticking down on the clock. "Three minutes should be just long enough."

"Long enough for what?"

"To kiss you."

She took an instinctive step back. "Or to finish clearing the table."

Jason shook his head. "That doesn't sound like nearly as much fun."

"Sometimes fun has to wait until the work is done."

"You're right," he decided, returning to the table. "And if I wait until later to kiss you, I won't have to worry about being interrupted by a buzzing kitchen timer."

"I've been thinking about the kissing thing," she admitted.

"I've been thinking about it, too—to the distraction of all else."

"What I was thinking," Alyssa said, determined to take control of the conversation, "is that there's really no reason for you to kiss me. I mean, it's not as if we have to demonstrate our technique to convince my parents that we're dating."

"Maybe not," he acknowledged. "But couples who have been dating for several months are usually pretty comfortable around one another. And aside from that night when you grabbed hold of me and practically hauled me across the bar to kiss me, every time I get close to you, you back away."

"Sorry," she said automatically. "I guess I'm a little protective of my personal space."

"If you expect anyone to believe that we're together, you're going to have to let me in."

She nodded. "You're right."

He watched her, waiting.

She drew a deep breath, as if shoring up her courage, and took a deliberate step toward him.

"I'm not so scary, am I?"

"Of course not," she said.

"So why is your heart racing?"

"It's not—"

"It is," he insisted, lifting a hand to touch the pulse point at the base of her jaw.

"It's just that… Actually, I don't know why my heart's racing," she admitted.

"I think you do know," he said. "You just don't want to admit it."

"Admit what?"

"That the attraction between us is getting harder and harder to ignore."

She swallowed. "But we agreed that we are going to ignore it."

"That would be the smart thing to do," he agreed.

But it wasn't what he wanted to do. For the first time, he wanted to ignore his own rules, take her in his arms and—

The buzz of the timer severed his thought.

## *Chapter Nine*

"I have a confession to make," Jay said when he picked up his fork to dig into the lava cake, dusted with powdered sugar and decorated with fresh raspberries.

Alyssa eyed him warily. "A confession along the lines of 'I'm not a big fan of raspberries' or more like 'I'm on the FBI's most wanted list'?"

"Somewhere in between those options, although definitely closer to the raspberries."

"Okay," she said.

"When you met my friends last weekend, did you sense any…friction?"

"You mean, between you and Kevin?"

"I'll take that as a yes," he said. "Well, me, Kevin, Carter and Matt all played high school football together."

"You've been friends for a long time," she noted.

"We have—aside from a brief period in our junior year when Kevin stopped talking to me."

"I'm guessing there was a girl."

He nodded. "Her name was Lacey Bolton. She wasn't a cheerleader or an athlete—she was just a pretty girl who sat in front of Kevin in English class."

"He had a crush on her," Alyssa guessed.

"And she had no idea he even existed, because she was more interested in school than boys. But Kevin was smart and patient, and he had a plan. He asked for her help with a term paper, and they started to get together for study sessions once a week.

"We all ribbed him about taking it slow, but it was obvious he really liked her and was gearing up to ask her to the homecoming dance."

"I've only been here for one homecoming," she acknowledged. "But I know what a big deal it is."

"Especially to the football players, who are in the spotlight all weekend. Win or lose, they're the heroes. All the guys want to play on the team, and all the girls want to go out with the players."

"You were quarterback," she guessed.

"First string," he confirmed. "But I got sacked in the season opener and went down with an ankle sprain. Gilmore took my place on the roster—and my girlfriend."

"Apparently there's some recent animosity between the Blakes and the Gilmores," she mused.

"Getting dumped was hard enough," he admitted. "Losing Jenny to Gilmore made it that much harder. Not only would I have to sit on the sidelines for the big game, I'd be sitting alone.

"And because I was feeling so crappy about the whole situation, I decided that gave me a free pass for crappy behavior."

"What did you do?" she asked, clearly anticipating something bad.

"I asked Lacey to be my date for the homecoming dance—and she said yes."

She winced. "How long did it take Kevin to forgive you?"

"A very long time," he admitted. "And recently I did something that brought it all back again."

"Made another move on Lacey Bolton?"

"No. I made a move on you."

She looked taken aback by his confession. "When did you make a move on me?"

"Well, technically, you made the move when you kissed me, but Kevin doesn't seem concerned with technicalities."

"You told your friend that I kissed you?"

"No," he denied. "But he was at The Daily Grind when Megan Carmichael told Kenzie Atkins that she saw me kissing you at Diggers'."

Alyssa sighed. "I guess I shouldn't have expected to kiss a guy in a public place and not have people take notice." She sipped her wine. "Do you want me to explain it to…Kevin?"

He shook his head. "I don't think that will help."

"So what was the purpose of telling me the story?" she wondered.

"He'd never admit it, but Kevin's a romantic," Jay told her. "And he seems willing to forgive what he sees as my betrayal if I can convince him that I was motivated by real feelings for you."

"If he's known you for so many years, shouldn't he know that you don't do real feelings?"

He arched a brow.

"Just stating what seems to be a well-known fact," she told him.

"Like I said, Kevin's a romantic. But to prove to him that this isn't another Lacey Bolton situation, I have to date you, exclusively, up to and including Matt's wedding."

"You're serious," she realized.

He nodded grimly.

"The seemingly out-of-the-blue invitation to your friend's wedding makes a little more sense now."

"You didn't believe that I just wanted you to be my date?"

She shook her head. "Guys like you don't make plans with a girl that far into the future, because you're never sure that you'll be with that same girl by the time the event comes around."

"That's a little harsh," he noted.

"Maybe it is," she acknowledged. "But I doubt it's untrue."

"Well, since we have a date two months into the future—and the meeting with your parents before then—we're going to need more practice."

She eyed him warily. "Kissing?"

He grinned. "That, too," he agreed. "But what I meant was just hanging out and being together."

"That's probably a good idea," she acknowledged.

"Do you have any plans tomorrow?" he asked.

She shook her head.

"Good. I should be finished work by three, so we'll plan to leave here around four," he decided.

"To go where?" she wondered.

"It's a surprise."

She narrowed her gaze. "Are you going to make me play laser tag or go rock climbing?"

"Those are both good ideas," he said. "But no—not tomorrow."

He'd already introduced her to paintball, and though she'd been apprehensive in the beginning—perhaps more about meeting his friends than potentially being hit by paintballs—she'd willingly geared up. Nat had given her a quick lesson on her weapon—how to load and aim and shoot—then spent some time with her at the target range before announcing that she was ready to go.

Alyssa had loved the game and, afterward, had shown off the various colorful bruises that were evidence of the hits she'd taken. He'd winced at the blue and yellow blemishes that marred her smooth skin, but she'd been proud of her battle scars. Having been held back from trying new things or pushing physical limits for so many years because her parents had worried—despite the doctors' reassurances—that her heart wasn't completely fixed, she seemed eager to do and try anything. Which, of course, made him wonder if she'd exhibit the same curiosity and eagerness in the bedroom—a prospect that was too torturous to contemplate for long.

Aside from the almost offhand admission that she'd been born with a hole in her heart, her medical condition wasn't something she talked about. And while he understood that the surgeries had happened a lot of years earlier and weren't likely at the forefront of her mind, he'd noticed that she always dressed in a way that ensured any remaining scars weren't visible.

Admittedly curious after the night that she'd bumped Carter from the Tetris leaderboard, he'd done an internet search of "atrial septal defect" and "heart surgery scars." What he'd learned had given him some appreciation for what Alyssa deemed overprotectiveness on the part of her parents, and renewed respect for the woman who had exhibited determination and courage in building a life for herself free of anyone else's restrictions.

"If you're not going to tell me where we're going, can you at least give me a hint as to what I should wear?" she asked him now.

"Whatever you want."

She huffed out a breath. "Could you be any less helpful?"

"Stiletto heels and a very short skirt," he suggested.

"Apparently you *can* be less helpful," she decided.

He grinned. "We're probably going to be outside, so wear something comfortable and appropriate for the weather."

"When you say outside, do you mean in a paintball field?"

He chuckled. "Not this time."

"Oh," she said.

And he thought she sounded almost disappointed.

It was May, but what was "appropriate for the weather" in northern Nevada was very different than Southern California. In Irvine, she would have packed her winter clothes away long ago. In Haven, though the sun provided welcome warmth during the day, temperatures tended to drop quickly and steeply when it went down.

After some consideration, Alyssa opted for a long-sleeved peasant-style blouse over a pair of slim-fitting pants with short, low-heeled boots. She used a light hand with her makeup and added a spritz of her favorite perfume.

Jason greeted her with a quick kiss.

He'd been kissing her a lot over the past few weeks, though the kisses had mostly just been casual brushes of his lips. And he'd been touching her frequently, too—holding her hand, draping an arm over her shoulders or just sitting close enough so that their bodies touched. And if his intent was to get her accustomed to those easy kisses and casual touches, she thought it was succeeding.

Unfortunately, instead of inuring her to the effects, her awareness of—and attraction to—him was growing every day, and she was starting to worry that she might get too used to these casual displays of affection and start to believe their phony relationship was real.

"Are you going to tell me now where we're going?" she asked after they'd been driving for several minutes.

"Twelve-oh-two Miners' Pass."

"That doesn't really answer my question," she noted.

"It very specifically answers your question," he argued.

"Okay—what is at twelve-oh-two Miners' Pass?" she asked.

"A house."

She rolled her eyes. "And do you happen to know who lives at this house?"

"As a matter of fact, I do."

She counted slowly to ten while she watched the scenery pass outside her window, but of course, he didn't offer any more information. "Are you going to tell me who lives at this house?"

"I am," he confirmed. "But not until we're a little closer to our destination, because I don't want you to freak out about meeting my parents."

"I don't freak out," she said, ignoring the knots that suddenly tightened in her belly. "And why am I meeting your parents?"

"It seemed reasonable that if I'm going to meet your parents, I should introduce you to mine."

"This wasn't part of our agreement."

"But it was your idea," he said. "When I suggested reciprocity, you asked if I wanted to introduce you to my parents."

"I was *joking.*"

"Well, I didn't know you were joking. And when my mom invited me to come over for a barbecue, I decided that having you there would increase the odds of the afternoon being tolerable.

"That sounded harsh," he realized. "And they're really not so bad. A little pretentious and self-absorbed at times, but generally friendly. Besides, it seemed like a good opportunity to give the boyfriend-girlfriend thing a trial run."

"What did you tell your parents about me?" she finally asked.

"Nothing."

"Did you even tell them that I was coming?"

"Nope."

He turned into a wide stamped-concrete driveway in front of a gorgeous three-story stone-and-brick house, the grandeur of which made her forget—for just a moment— the topic of their conversation.

"I really don't think this is a good idea," she said when he killed the engine.

He exited the truck and came around to open her door, reaching across to unsnap her seat belt when she made no move to do so herself.

"Relax, honey bear. We're just here for a burger. My mom's a horrible cook, but my dad does a decent job with meat over fire."

"I'm not sure I believe you," Alyssa said, ignoring the teasing endearment.

"It's true," a female voice said from behind him. "Our mother could scorch a pot attempting to boil water."

Alyssa stepped out of the vehicle and turned to face a woman who could only be Jason's sister. Average height, slender build, light blond hair, deep blue eyes like her brother's and the same quick smile. Regan, she guessed, since he'd told her that Brielle lived in New York and rarely returned to Haven.

Of course, Alyssa had been doubting his reasons for bringing her here, not the truth of his culinary commentary, but she didn't have a chance to clarify as Jason was already making the introductions.

"It's nice to meet you." Instead of offering a hand, Regan gave Alyssa a quick hug. Then she turned to her brother to remark, "And surprising, because you don't have that blank look in your eyes that Jay usually favors in the women he dates."

"Try to make a good first impression," he said. "Oh, wait—too late."

Regan just grinned, unrepentant, and hooked her arm through Alyssa's. "Come on," she said. "Everyone's dying to meet you."

"But—" She looked helplessly back at Jason.

"I didn't tell Mom and Dad that I was bringing a guest," he noted.

"But you told me," Regan reminded him.

"My mistake, obviously," he noted.

"You know how Mom is about surprises," his sister said. "And if she found out that I knew about Alyssa and didn't tell her, she'd never forgive me."

"You mean she'd be annoyed with you, for all of about thirty seconds."

"I'm a middle child—desperate for approval," she said by way of explanation.

"You're the second oldest and a troublemaker," he countered.

"Actually, I'm 'the smart one,'" Regan told Alyssa, using air quotes. "Jason's 'the stubborn one,' Spencer's 'the slippery one' and Brie's 'the sweet one.'"

Alyssa wondered if her own parents had ever described her and Cristina in similarly generic terms. If they had, she had no doubt what they would be. Her sister was "the perfect one" and she was "the broken one."

But she didn't feel broken when she was with Jason.

When she was with him, she felt not just like a normal person but an attractive and desirable woman. And she knew that regardless of how or when they put an end to their relationship charade, she would always be grateful to him for that.

Jason's mention of burgers implied a casual meal. But apparently dining with Ben and Margaret Channing meant eating off gold-rimmed plates at an enormous table in the formal dining room lit by a chandelier that wouldn't have looked out of place in a hotel ballroom.

"And what is it that you do, dear?" Margaret asked Alyssa as she spooned coleslaw out of a crystal bowl, using a fancy slotted spoon that looked like real silver.

Alyssa added a slice of tomato to her burger. "I'm a math and science teacher at Westmount High School."

"I loved math, hated science," Regan said.

"Even physics?" Alyssa asked her.

"I didn't take physics," she admitted. "My guidance counsellor steered me toward chemistry."

"If you like math—and obviously you do," she said, remembering that Jason's sister was an accountant, "you'd like physics."

"Our youngest daughter, Brielle, is a teacher," Ben said.

Alyssa nodded. "Jason mentioned that she lives in New York."

"And teaches at a prestigious private school in Brooklyn," Margaret confirmed. "In fact, they've already offered to renew her contract for next year."

"That's good news," Jay said.

His parents exchanged a look.

"She loves teaching at Briarwood," Regan reminded them.

"Which would be great, if Briarwood wasn't twenty-five hundred miles away." Margaret shook her head. "We should never have agreed to let her go to New York City."

"We couldn't have stopped her," her husband pointed out. "She was eighteen—and determined to put as much distance as possible between herself and Haven."

"We didn't have to make it easy for her."

"I don't think it was easy," Ben said.

"I mean financially," Margaret clarified. "We paid her tuition and all her living expenses."

"Same as we did for each of our other children."

"Except Spencer," Regan chimed in. "Who decided he'd rather ride bareback than read or write."

"Our youngest son left college to become a professional cowboy," Ben explained to Alyssa.

"At least you know Brie's got great roommates and a nice apartment," Jay pointed out. "Spencer lives out of a suitcase, and more than half the time, you don't even know where that suitcase is."

"But he's been very successful," Margaret said to Alyssa. "After dinner, you should let Jason take you into the den and show you some of Spencer's trophies."

"Yeah, because that's going to score him points with his girlfriend," Regan said mockingly. "Showing her his little brother's hardware."

"Jason won his share of trophies, too," Margaret said, though her defense of her oldest son was a little tepid.

"For throwing a football around," Regan said.

"He also graduated summa cum laude with a degree in business," Ben said. "Which would make him a real asset at Blake Mining."

"Can we possibly have one family meal where we don't rehash the same arguments?" Jason asked wearily.

"I'm sure that degree is one of the reasons he's made

Adventure Village such a success in a short time," Alyssa remarked.

Ben let out a derisive snort. "He bought an empty field where fake soldiers shoot at each other with fake guns."

She could sense Jason seething and reached over to put her hand on his arm. "Paintball might not be everyone's idea of a good time," she acknowledged. "But it's certainly popular with a lot of people."

"Teenagers," Ben said dismissively.

"Who, according to the teachers at Westmount, finally have something to do with their time other than tagging buildings and stealing cars."

"And it's not just paintball," Regan pointed out. "There's also laser tag and a climbing wall."

"And mini golf," Alyssa added.

"It's a fine hobby," Ben finally allowed. "I'm just saying that Jason's time and talent would be put to better use at Blake Mining."

"I worked at Blake Mining for six years," Jay reminded his father. "In the mines, in the lab, in the office—and I hated every job."

"If work was supposed to be fun, it wouldn't be called work," his father said.

"Dessert?" Margaret spoke up quickly to interrupt what was apparently a familiar dispute.

"You made dessert?" Regan asked cautiously.

"Of course not," her mother said, as if the very idea was ridiculous. "Celeste prepared everything we need for strawberry shortcake. I just have to put it together."

"I'll give you a hand," her daughter offered.

"Sorry about the side of family drama served with your burger," Jay said to Alyssa as they drove home from his parents' house.

"I'm not unfamiliar with family conflict," she reminded him. "And while your dad clearly wishes you'd chosen a career in a different direction, your mom seems happy with your choices."

"I don't know if she's happy or just unwilling to express her displeasure, in case I decide to follow in the footsteps of Spencer or Brie."

"Did you ever want to leave Haven?" she asked curiously.

"Sure. When I was a teenager and there was nothing to do, I hated this town and promised myself I'd get out at the first opportunity. So imagine my surprise when I went away to school and discovered that I actually missed it. That got me thinking about why I wanted to leave and what would make me—and a lot more people like me—want to stay."

"And that's how Adventure Village started?"

"I guess it was," he admitted. "Well, the idea plus the trust fund from my grandfather."

He pulled into their shared driveway and parked.

"I'm going to sit outside for a while," he said. "I usually need to clear my head after too much time with my family."

"Three hours is too much time?"

"By about two hours," he confirmed.

"Do you want some company?" Alyssa asked.

"I wouldn't mind."

"Just let me go in and grab a sweater," she said.

"No need," he told her. "I've got one in my duffel bag in the back—it's clean, I promise."

He opened the back door, unzipped the bag and pulled out the sweatshirt. She tugged it over her head.

His lips twitched as he helped her roll back the cuffs to free her hands. The bear logo covered her chest and the hem fell to midthigh. "I guess it's a little big."

"But it's warm." She glanced down at the crest. "My sister went to UC Berkeley, too."

"Where'd you go to school?"

"UC Irvine," she replied.

"You didn't want to go away?" he asked.

"I desperately wanted to go away," she admitted. "But my mom worried about me being too far from the doctors who knew my medical history."

"How'd she react when you told her you were moving to Nevada?" he wondered.

"She wasn't thrilled—and even less so when she realized the nearest hospital was thirty-five miles away and didn't have a cardiologist on staff."

"You weren't worried?"

She shook her head. "No, because I believed the doctors who said my heart is fine. I don't need constant reassurances or reminders of something that happened a long time ago."

Maybe it was the dark. Maybe it was that he knew her better than he had a few weeks earlier and felt comfortable enough now to be able to voice the question that had been on his mind since she told him about her surgery.

Whatever the reason, he finally asked, "Is that why you hide your scars?"

## Chapter Ten

Jay felt her stiffen beside him, and he wondered if no one else had ever asked her the question. But after a barely perceptible hesitation, Alyssa said, "I hide my scars because they're ugly."

He scowled into the darkness. "Who told you they're ugly?"

"I didn't need to be told—I've seen them."

But he knew her well enough now to sense that there was more to the story, and he hated to think that anyone had ever made this strong, beautiful woman feel as if she was anything less than that.

"Show me," he said gently.

She immediately shook her head. "I don't think so."

"I know you're probably thinking I just want to get a closer look at your breasts, but that's only part of the reason."

She smiled. "I'm going to change the subject now and tell you that I had a good time tonight."

And because he'd never wanted to make her uncomfortable, he followed her lead. "I did, too—for the most part."

"Does your mom really not cook?" she asked curiously.

"She really doesn't," he confirmed. "I ate a lot of pizza and cold cereal growing up."

She looked so horrified, he had to laugh. "I'm kidding. Not about my mother not cooking—that's the truth. But Celeste, the housekeeper-slash-nanny, made sure there was a hot meal on the table every night."

"We really do come from different worlds," she noted. "And, in my world, morning comes early."

"I should be more aware of school nights when I'm dating a teacher," he remarked.

"Fake dating," she reminded him.

Except that this pretend relationship with Alyssa was starting to feel more real to Jay than anything else he'd experienced in a long time.

After dinner with Jason's family, Alyssa got the sense that something had changed in their relationship. She'd seen a side of him she'd never noticed before, observed some interesting family dynamics and glimpsed vulnerabilities she never would have guessed lurked beneath his veneer of self-confidence. And the more she learned about him, the more she liked him.

Of course, watching him with his parents and sister, she also couldn't help but compare his family to her own. She hadn't grown up with the kind of wealth that was evident in every brick of their home and every designer thread on his mother's back, but she'd never had cause to doubt the love or support of her family.

Which only made her feel guiltier about her deception. And the closer it got to the date of her parents' visit, the more nervous she was about introducing them to her boyfriend. She wanted them to like Jason, though she knew it didn't really matter whether they did or didn't, so long as they believed Alyssa liked him.

And she did.

She was also powerfully attracted to him.

Spending time with Jason, being touched and kissed by him, made her body ache for so much more. Maybe she didn't fully appreciate the pleasures that could be shared by a man and a woman, but she yearned to know. And with each day that passed, that yearning continued to grow.

"When are your parents getting in?" Jason's question drew her back to the present as they hit the halfway mark of their run Friday morning.

"Their flight is scheduled to land just after two o'clock tomorrow afternoon."

"We've got a big event on Saturday, but I can ask Matt to cover for me, if you want me to go to the airport with you."

"No," she immediately responded. "I appreciate the offer, and I know my mother's primary incentive for making this trip is to meet you, but I think it's probably best to limit the amount of time you spend with them."

"You don't think I can be a convincing boyfriend?" he challenged.

"I want to minimize the opportunities for missteps."

"So when am I going to meet them?"

"About ten minutes before we leave to go to The Hide-Away for dinner Saturday night."

"I thought you were going to make a reservation at Diggers'."

"I was," she admitted. "And then I realized that it was less likely we'd face questions from friends and neighbors if we went out of town."

"Well, if we're going into Battle Mountain, El Aguila

would have been my choice," he remarked. "They have the best burritos north of Mexico."

"You only think so because you haven't had my grandmother's burritos," she told him.

"Have you ever been to El Aguila?" he asked.

"I can't say that I have," she admitted.

"Then we'll have to go sometime."

"I'd like that, but…"

"But what?" he prompted.

"I think you're forgetting that, after this weekend, you won't have to be my pretend boyfriend anymore."

"But you still have to be my pretend girlfriend until Matt's wedding."

"The original agreement was simply for me to be your date."

"I like this girlfriend-boyfriend arrangement better," he told her. "But even when it's done, we'll still be friends, won't we?"

"I guess we will," she acknowledged.

"And we'll go to El Aguila," he promised.

"Okay," she agreed. "But right now, we need to kick it up a notch or I'm going to be late for school."

"When you say things like that, I feel like I'm a teenager again. Although back then, the math teacher only *wished* she was dating me."

She sent him a sideways glance. "Really? Because Carter told me you had Mr. Donald for math in high school."

He responded by kicking it up several notches, leaving her in his dust.

But she was laughing.

Before Jason headed to Adventure Village Saturday afternoon, he showed up at Alyssa's door with a six-pack of his favorite brew and a framed photo of himself in climbing gear, hanging off the edge of a cliff. Though he was obviously wearing a harness, the image still made her stomach dip as if she was the one suspended in midair.

She looked from the photo back to the man. "Thank you?"

He shook his head. "Doesn't a woman usually want a picture of her boyfriend around so she can look at it when she's not with him? And his favorite beer in her fridge so that he'll want to stop by for a drink?"

"They're props," she realized.

"All part of the service," he told her.

She tucked the beer in her fridge and put the picture on her desk, beside her computer monitor. She picked up the sweatshirt she'd borrowed and carried it back to the foyer.

"I almost forgot you had that," he admitted when she handed him the freshly laundered and folded garment.

"I wanted to wash it before I returned it," she said.

"Appreciated but not necessary," he told her. "And maybe you should keep it for a few more days."

"Why?"

"Another prop to add to the relationship illusion," he pointed out. "The boyfriend's sweatshirt, casually discarded over the back of a chair."

"My mother would be appalled that I hadn't tidied up before their visit."

"Maybe neatly folded on top of your laundry basket, then," he suggested.

"A much better idea," she agreed, taking back the garment.

"Have you checked their flight status?"

She nodded. "Everything's on schedule."

"So when are you heading out to the airport?"

"In about ten minutes."

"That isn't a lot of time, but I can work with it," he said and hauled her into his arms to kiss her.

He'd kissed her often enough over the past few weeks that she should be accustomed to the feel of his lips on hers by now. But still her heart raced and mind blanked.

Every. Single. Time.

She had no defense against the sensual assault of his mouth. She wanted none.

She only wanted Jason.

And yet he always seemed completely in control. He occasionally did a little tactile exploring while she was being thoroughly seduced by his lips, but always through the barrier of fabric. His ruthless restraint tempted her to abandon her own. To shed not just her inhibitions but every stitch of clothing to feel his hands on her bare skin. His body against hers.

It was almost embarrassing how much she wanted him. So far, she'd managed to resist begging him to take her, but the words echoed temptingly in her mind as he continued to kiss her. The sensual flick of his tongue sent flames of heat licking through her veins, making every part of her burn.

"If I don't leave now, we're both going to be late," he said after he'd eased his lips from hers.

"Late?" she echoed.

That incredibly talented mouth curved. "That's what was missing."

"What?" How was she supposed to concentrate on what he was saying when her head was spinning?

"Now when you meet your parents, you'll look like a woman who's thinking about her man," he said.

Of course, he wasn't really her man, but the whole point of this weekend was to convince her parents that he was. The harder task would be remembering that it was just a game they were playing and not letting him into her fragile heart.

* * *

Alyssa was more apprehensive than she'd expected to be about her parents meeting Jason—not just because she worried that they'd uncover her deception, but because she really wanted them to like him. Renata seemed invested in the idea of her youngest daughter falling in love with Diego, and Alyssa worried that her mother might have already decided she wasn't going to like Jason. Although she believed Miguel was less likely to prejudge her beau, she felt anxious anyway.

Her parents were reserved but not unfriendly, and over dinner, they all chatted easily. Her father seemed sincerely interested in Jason's business and asked all the questions about Adventure Village she knew his own father had not. And when her mother expressed curiosity about the battle that had given the town its name, Jason sketched out a brief history lesson that hit all the important highlights.

Any concerns Alyssa had that Jason might try to oversell their relationship proved groundless. He was attentive without being too obvious and deferential without being submissive. While they were eating, he snagged a mushroom from her plate, as if it was common for them to share food; as they walked across the parking lot, he linked their fingers together, as if the casual gesture was an ingrained habit.

After they returned to Haven and the triplex where they both lived—a revelation that created a furrow between Renata's brows—they sat outside for a while to enjoy the starry night. Jason introduced her dad to "Icky" while Alyssa and her mom each had a glass of wine.

When Miguel said he was tired and heading to bed, Renata, of course, went with him, leaving Alyssa and Jason sitting out on the deck under the stars twinkling in the sky.

He moved closer, putting his arm around her and pulling her against his body.

"What are you doing?" she asked him.

"Snuggling with my honey bear."

She rolled her eyes. "Why?"

He put his mouth next to her ear, as if whispering sweet nothings. "In case they're peeking out the window."

The warmth of his breath raised goose bumps on her skin and heated her blood. "You think my parents are spying on us?"

"I think, if they have any doubts about our relationship, they might be looking for evidence of a deception."

"My mother's interrogation over dinner wasn't very subtle, was it?" she asked, struggling to stay focused on their conversation—not an easy task when her hormones, stirred up by his proximity, were clamoring for action.

"I think I handled her questions pretty well. But I also think, even if they're one hundred percent convinced, they would expect their daughter's boyfriend to take advantage of their absence to steal a few kisses—maybe even cop a feel."

She laughed, as he no doubt intended her to do.

"I'm thinking that this pretend dating thing might be better than real dating," she told him.

"Why would you say that?" he wondered.

"Because it's fun without the pressure and expectations."

"It has been fun," he agreed. "But it hasn't been easy."

"I know you've had to do a lot of juggling of your schedule this weekend," she acknowledged. "And I'm sincerely grateful."

"My schedule was the least of it."

"What do you mean?"

He shook his head. "It's my problem, not yours."

"Except that I dragged you into this," she reminded him.

"I wasn't completely unwilling."

"Obviously we have different recollections of how this all began," she remarked wryly.

"I wasn't completely unwilling *after* the chicken marsala," he amended. "Despite the fact that you made me eat asparagus."

She smiled as she tipped her head back against his shoulder. "You're a good sport, Jason Channing."

"I would have said 'savvy negotiator.'"

"We can go with that," she agreed. "But I think I got the better end of the deal."

"Just make sure you've got July 14 marked on your calendar."

"What's the— Oh, right. Your friend's wedding."

"For which you're my plus-one," he reminded her.

"Only because Kevin backed you into a corner."

But Jay knew that wasn't entirely true.

Maybe Kevin's challenge had been the reason for the initial invitation, but there wasn't anyone else he wanted to take to Matt's wedding. After only three weeks, he was tempted to abandon the pretense. Because this make-believe relationship was more real than anything he'd had in a long time.

Or maybe he just wanted to think that was true, to alleviate any lingering guilt over the fact that he'd kissed the girl that one of his best friends had been crushing on.

Or maybe he was just tempted to think they could make a real relationship work because their fake dating had been, as she'd noted, fun. On the other hand, he suspected it had been fun only because he hadn't been thinking about how to get her into bed. In fact, he'd been trying very hard *not* to think about Alyssa in his bed.

Instead, he focused on the purpose of their charade. It was all about deception: Alyssa wanted her parents to believe she was in a relationship so they wouldn't worry about her living so far away—and so her mother would stop trying to set her up with other guys; and Jay was willing to play along because pretending to be infatuated with his neighbor had seemed the quickest way to earn forgiveness from Kevin.

And so far, it *had* been fun. Except for the cold showers. Those had not been fun, and he'd been suffering through them before bed almost every night—and frequently after running with her in the mornings, too.

But as uncomfortable as it was to stand beneath the icy spray, it was necessary. Because as much as he wanted to explore the attraction that simmered between them, he didn't dare make a real move. If he ever got naked with a woman who was his neighbor and a friend, it would be all kinds of awkward when the relationship ended.

The possibility of a mutually satisfying relationship that didn't end never crossed his mind, because he didn't do happily-ever-after. He didn't even do long-term. Maybe someday, but he wasn't ready to settle down just yet.

But the more time Jay spent with Alyssa, the more he realized he didn't want anyone else, and that realization made him uneasy. Thankfully, her parents were going back to California the next day, and the status quo would be restored.

Jason showed up at Alyssa's door just after lunch on Monday to accompany her and her parents to the airport. She was grateful to have his company for the trip back, not to mention that the action scored major points with her mother. They stood together and watched Renata and Miguel go through the security line.

"That wasn't so bad, was it?" he asked.

"Only the longest three days of my life," she said, waving to her mom and dad as they disappeared from view.

"But at least it's done now and we can go back to our respective lives as if this weekend never happened." Her tone was upbeat, but she couldn't deny that the prospect left her feeling a little disappointed.

"Just when I was getting the hang of this boyfriend thing," he lamented.

"You were the perfect boyfriend," she confirmed.

"Handsome? Attentive? Charming?"

"All of the above," she agreed with a smile. "But most important—temporary."

He stared at her. "You really aren't looking for a relationship?"

"Why does everyone seem so surprised by that? Why is it okay for a man to not want to be tied down, but a woman is always expected to want a husband and a family?"

"Are you saying that you don't want a husband and a family?"

"Well, sure I do, someday," she admitted. "I'm just not in any hurry for it to happen."

"In that case, you just might be the perfect girlfriend," he decided.

"Look at us—a match made in heaven."

"Haven," he corrected.

She laughed. "But on a more serious note, thank you, sincerely, for this weekend."

"It's not quite over yet," he noted. "And I'm hungry."

"You need to work on your subtlety," she told him.

He shook his head. "I'm not trying to wrangle another meal from you."

"You're not?" Her tone was skeptical.

"In fact, I was thinking of cooking for you—if grilling counts as cooking," he clarified. "We can pick up a couple of steaks, some potatoes, open a bottle of wine and celebrate the conclusion of a successful weekend."

"I appreciate the offer," she told him. And she was undeniably tempted, but—

"I don't want to hear any 'buts,'" he said.

She closed her mouth, reconsidered her words and tried again. "However—"

"Nope." He cut her off. "'However' is the same as 'but' just with more syllables, so I don't want to hear that, either."

"What do you want to hear?"

"Something along the lines of 'that sounds like a great idea and I would love to have dinner with you' would work."

"That sounds like a great idea and I would love to have dinner with you," she dutifully intoned.

"That wasn't so hard now, was it?"

"No," she admitted. "I just expected that, after all the time we've spent together over the past few weeks, you'd be grateful to have some space."

He shrugged. "It turns out I don't mind having you in my space."

She put a hand on her chest. "Oh, Jason—you're *such* a romantic."

He grinned. "Let me know if you're going to swoon, so I can get in position to catch you."

"Unless we travel back in time two hundred years, I'm not going to swoon," she assured him.

"Modern women don't swoon?"

"No more than contemporary men solve disagreements with pistols at dawn."

"We prefer paintball at dusk," he acknowledged.

"Speaking of which—are you sure you don't want to head back to Adventure Village?"

"Hmm…let me think about that." He tapped a finger against his chin. "Hanging out with a bunch of sweaty guys or some one-on-one time with a pretty girl…that is a tough choice." He took her hand. "But I choose you."

## *Chapter Eleven*

So they picked up steaks and potatoes. Alyssa threw together a salad with ingredients she had in her fridge and they dined on his deck.

"You were right," she said as Jay emptied the last of the wine into her glass.

"Words a man always likes to hear," he remarked. "But what, specifically, was I right about?"

"I do hide my scars."

"I know that," he said, wondering what had caused her to introduce the topic now. Was she feeling relaxed because the weekend had gone so well? Or was it possible that she'd grown to like and trust him? Or maybe her confession was simply an aftereffect of three glasses of wine. "But I don't know why."

"Partly it's because old habits die hard," she admitted. "My mother always made sure the clothes she bought for me didn't let the scars show. She never made a big deal about them, and I know it's not because she thinks they're unsightly, but because they're a reminder to her that I almost died."

"Is there another part?" he asked gently.

"Mean girls and beach day in my senior year of high school."

"Mean girls are usually mean because they're jealous."

She nodded. "And I was dating Craig Gerber. He wasn't on the football team, but he was class president. Smart, good-looking and extremely popular. Not the type of guy who would ordinarily look twice at me. In fact, we'd been in classes together since junior high, and he didn't even know my name until tenth grade."

"What happened then?"

"I got boobs."

He sighed appreciatively. "Those do tend to catch a teenage boy's attention—and often a man's, too."

She smiled at that. "Well, a result of that hormonal spurt, I was no longer the shy, skinny girl who hid out in the library but the shy girl with the boobs who hid out in the library.

"And one day, Craig Gerber came into the library and asked me to have lunch with him."

"And suddenly you were dating Craig Gerber," he guessed.

"There was nothing sudden about it. I was very shy and more than a little oblivious. And there were so many girls who wanted to be with him, it never occurred to me that he could want me—until he asked me to be his date for prom.

"Of course, I said yes." She smiled, a little wistfully, at the memory. "My mother took me shopping for a new dress and shoes and made appointments for me to have my hair and nails done. That night was everything I had dreamed it could be. We danced and we kissed and we stayed out late.

"Then there was a breakfast for grads back at the high

school the next day, and after that, everyone headed to the beach." Her words were a little more clipped now, as if she was in a hurry to finish the story. "Most of the other girls were sunbathing in their teeny, tiny bikinis, and I was wearing one, too, but with a cover-up. They encouraged me to take off the shirt and catch some rays, but I wasn't comfortable baring so much skin—or my scars—in front of everyone there.

"When I continued to resist, Tiffany Butler accused me of being a prude, and Amie Myers said 'You don't have anything the rest of us don't have.'"

Her gaze dropped away. He wanted to reassure her that he didn't need to hear all the unpleasant details, but he sensed that she needed to tell them, so he remained silent, waiting for her to continue.

"But Amie knew about my scars because we were friends when we were little," she confided. "I'd slept over at her house and she'd slept over at mine, so I thought—" She shook her head, as if berating herself. "I actually thought she was trying to reassure me that the scars weren't a big deal."

He touched a hand to her arm, a silent gesture of support and encouragement.

Alyssa forged ahead. "I hadn't considered that, although we'd been close as kids, we'd grown apart over the years. She was outgoing and popular, and I was not—at least not until Craig Gerber started hanging out with me. And one of Amie's new BFFs was Tiffany, who'd been trying to snag Craig's attention for months and was not happy that he'd asked me to the prom.

"Anyway, encouraged by Amie's comment, I took off my shirt." She closed her eyes, and he knew she was clearly envisioning that moment, that day, and his heart ached for the pain he knew she was reliving.

"I didn't think my scars were gruesome, or even particularly noticeable," she said quietly, "but when Tiffany saw my chest, she screamed—a total drama queen shriek of horror that, of course, drew everyone's attention."

Now Jay was clearly envisioning it, too, and he hated imagining how horrible that experience was for her. If he'd been there… But, of course, he hadn't been. And there was nothing he could do to change what had happened in the past; he could only be here for her now.

"And then she pretended to be embarrassed by her reaction and 'apologized'—" Alyssa put air quotes around the word "—and said that she didn't blame me for wanting to conceal my hideous scars.

"I was tempted to ask about *her* surgery, since we all knew that she'd had a nose job as her graduation present from her parents."

"But you didn't," he said. It wasn't a question. He knew she would never be cruel or spiteful, though he couldn't help wishing that another one of her classmates had made the point.

"No, I didn't," she confirmed. "I just put my cover-up back on."

And had undoubtedly been covering up her scars ever since.

"What happened with Craig?" he asked.

"He was a little weirded out by the scars—or maybe by the idea of someone having a hole in their heart—though he pretended not to be. And when he took me home at the end of the day, he kissed me goodbye without trying to sneak his hands under my top and said 'See ya.' He hooked up with Tiffany before the end of the summer."

"Sounds like they deserved each other."

"Anyway," she said briskly, "that's the story. Since then, I have to really know and trust someone before I let them see my scars."

Jay couldn't blame her for that. On the other hand, she'd been carrying some pretty heavy baggage since high school and maybe it was time for her to let go of it.

"That's your choice, obviously. I just think…"

His train of thought completely jumped the track when he realized that her fingers were unfastening the buttons that ran down the front of her shirt.

She stood up and turned to face him, though she held the two sides of the shirt together, covering herself.

He swallowed. "What are you doing, Lys?"

"Proving that I trust you."

And then she pulled the shirt open, revealing lots of smooth, pale skin and full, round breasts cradled by cups of pale pink lace. All the blood in his head rapidly migrated south.

He swallowed again and reminded himself that she wasn't really baring her body but rather her soul.

He knew where to look for the scar and forced himself to focus on the thin, pale line that ran down the center of her chest, between those perfect breasts.

Perfectly motionless breasts, which clued him in to the fact that she was holding her breath. Waiting.

He finally lifted his gaze to hers and held it for a long moment without speaking.

She moistened her lips with the tip of her tongue. "You're not saying anything," she noted. "You're not shrieking, but you're not saying anything, either."

"I'm afraid to say the wrong thing," he admitted. "I want to tell you that you're beautiful, because you are, but even in my head, that sounds inadequate.

"I want to say thank you, for trusting me enough to take a step that I know wasn't easy for you to take.

"And I feel compelled to suggest that you cover yourself up again now, because I don't trust myself not to strip away the rest of your clothes to perform a close and very personal inspection of your gorgeous body."

Alyssa immediately tugged the sides of her shirt back together.

"Probably a wise move," Jason acknowledged, "though a disappointing one."

Her fingers fumbled as she tried to slide the buttons back through the holes.

He brushed her hands away to take over the task, but he stopped just past the halfway point, leaving the top four buttons unfastened.

Then he leaned forward and pressed his lips to the exposed skin above her breasts.

The kiss was unexpectedly sweet…and began the healing of old wounds deep inside.

She cleared her throat and attempted to lighten the mood. "I'm not going to sit here with my shirt only half buttoned."

"You can button it all the way to your throat if you want," he said. "Now that I know what you're wearing underneath, that's what I'm going to see in my mind when I look at you."

"And look at the time," she said.

"You're not really going to rush off already, are you?"

She nodded. "I've still got some work to do tonight. There's only a couple more weeks of school, then final exams and report cards to write."

Plus, she was starting to have real feelings for her sexy neighbor, so she told herself it was a good thing that the charade had come to an end.

And she almost believed it.

Of course, Alyssa's resolution to put some distance between them wasn't likely to get very far when he showed up to run with her the next day at 6:00 a.m. And every morning after that throughout the week.

But the running was routine for both of them, and the more miles they covered, the more confident she was that they'd returned to familiar—and safe—ground. She had a lot of fond memories of the time they'd spent together—from adrenaline-pumping rounds of laser tag to relaxing dinners in her apartment, from the bells and whistles of the arcade to quiet nights and long conversations under the stars, from casual hand-holding to bone-melting kisses.

She packed those memories away in the back of her mind so that she could focus on living in the present. Unfortunately, that mental exercise failed to alleviate the wanting that continued to churn inside her.

"I picked up a bag of frozen shrimp and some of that twisty pasta when I was at The Trading Post yesterday," he said as they neared the end of their route Friday morning. "I was hoping you might show me how to make the dish you were telling me about."

"You want a cooking lesson?" She couldn't help sounding dubious.

"If you don't mind."

Of course she didn't mind, but she also knew that she shouldn't agree. She was trying to put some much-needed distance between them, and spending one-on-one time in his kitchen was not the way to do that. But instead of refusing his request, she heard herself ask, "Do you have any ingredients other than the shrimp and pasta?"

"What else do I need?"

She shook her head despairingly. "When do you want this lesson?"

"Tonight? Tomorrow?" He shrugged. "Whenever you're available."

"I usually work Fridays," she reminded him. "But Duke

asked me to take the Saturday shift this weekend, so I could do tonight."

"Great," he said, sounding pleased by her response. "My place at seven?"

"Okay," she agreed.

And floated through the rest of her day looking forward to seven o'clock.

When she got home from school, she printed up a copy of the recipe and packed up a box with her sauté pan, pasta pot, colander, spatula, slotted spoon, garlic press, olive oil, canned tomatoes, fresh spinach, onion, garlic and red pepper flakes.

Jason raised his brows at the box when he opened the door.

"You said you had the pasta and the shrimp—I wasn't sure what else I'd be able to find in your kitchen," she explained.

"That was probably a good call," he acknowledged. "Although I did pick up a bottle of your favorite pinot noir and dessert from Sweet Caroline's Sweets."

Her gaze immediately went to the white bakery box on the counter. "What's for dessert?"

"You'll find out after you eat your dinner," he told her.

She smiled, recognizing the reversal of their roles in the conversation. "Okay, let's get this lesson started."

She set the recipe on the counter, then began to assemble the ingredients, faltering when she neared the end of the list.

"I forgot the basil."

"Do you need me to run to the store?" he offered.

"No, I meant I forgot it downstairs." She dumped the bag of frozen shrimp into the colander. "Run cold water over these to defrost them—I'll be right back."

Forty minutes later, they were sitting at the table with their pasta.

"It looks fabulous," Alyssa told him.

"I didn't think you'd let me screw it up."

She laughed. "So why are you looking at it as if you're afraid to try it?"

"Because you put green stuff in it."

"The green stuff was in the recipe," she pointed out, raising her own fork to her lips.

He watched as she chewed, swallowed.

Then she reached for her glass and raised it toward him. "Congratulations, Jason Channing—you cooked a delicious meal and it was not on a grill."

He sipped his wine, then finally sampled the pasta.

"It is good," he said, looking surprised—and a little proud.

They chatted about various topics while they finished their meal, including triple chocolate mousse cake for dessert. After clearing up the kitchen, Jason suggested that they take the rest of the wine onto his balcony.

"This view never gets old," she said, lowering herself onto the cushioned teak sofa beside him. "I wish I'd known about this when my parents were here—my mother would love this."

"Oh…um, that reminds me—she called earlier."

She froze with her glass halfway to her lips. "My mother called you?"

"No, she called your cell—when you ran downstairs to get the basil."

"Oh." She relaxed again and glanced at her watch. "I'll call her back when I go downstairs."

"Actually, she said that they were going to Cristina's tonight and that she'd talk to you tomorrow."

"You answered my phone?"

"Should I have let it go to voice mail?"

"No, it's fine," she said. "And now she can enjoy her visit with my sister without worrying that I didn't answer because I'd fallen and cracked my head open in the shower."

"If that's a real concern, I'm willing to spot you in the shower, honey bear."

She rolled her eyes at the deliberately provocative endearment as she shook her head. "Of course it's not a real concern—it's just one of those scenarios my mother dreams up when I'm not immediately accessible to her."

"Is that a yes or a no to watching you bathe?"

"A definite no," she said firmly.

"Because they say that more than thirty percent of household accidents occur in the bathroom."

"Who's they?" she challenged, reaching for her glass.

He shrugged. "Whoever keeps track of household accidents?"

She shook her head as she sipped her wine.

"During our brief conversation, your mom also happened to mention that it's their thirty-fifth wedding anniversary in a few weeks."

"It is," she confirmed. "Though I'm not sure why she'd mention it to you."

"She, uh, wanted to know if I was going to make the trip to California with you for the big celebration."

"And you told her that, unfortunately, you couldn't take the time away from work," she prompted.

"She caught me off guard," he admitted.

She frowned at his response. "You didn't… Jason, please say you didn't tell her that you would be there."

His gaze shifted away, a sure sign that she wasn't going to like his response. "I couldn't think of any reason not to."

"Work? Family obligations? A previous commitment?" She effortlessly tossed out the possibilities. "Pick one."

"You're right—I should have made up an excuse," he acknowledged. "And maybe I would have, but then she pointed out that it would be the perfect opportunity for the rest of your family to meet me."

"They only want to meet you because they think you're my boyfriend," she reminded him.

"Wasn't that the plan?"

She shook her head, beyond frustrated with him and the situation. "I only wanted you to meet them," she said. "*One meeting* so that my mother could stop worrying—and matchmaking."

"She doesn't seem to be matchmaking anymore," he said helpfully.

"And while I'm grateful for that, you are *not* coming with me to California," she asserted. Because she knew that spending ten days in close proximity to the man she was pretend dating would likely result in the development of real feelings. Especially when she was already fighting a daily battle against the physical attraction between them.

And maybe there were moments that she wondered *what if* she went to bed with him—and found herself tempted and tantalized by the possibilities. But so far, she'd managed to hold out against her own growing desire, because she knew that falling for "Charming" wouldn't lead to anything but heartache.

"I should have found a way to get you out of this," Alyssa said as they crossed the state line into California.

"You didn't get me into it," Jay reminded her.

"If I hadn't kissed you in front of Diego, my parents wouldn't have come to Haven to meet my supposed boyfriend, and they certainly wouldn't have invited you to their anniversary party," she pointed out.

"I like California," he said easily. And while it was true, it wasn't the reason he'd agreed to make this trip.

Not that he'd taken the time to examine his motivations

too closely, perhaps because he wasn't quite ready to admit the truth—even to himself. But he could admit that he wanted to know her better, and seeing Alyssa within the circle of her extended family seemed like the perfect opportunity to gain a deeper understanding of who she was and what she wanted.

"Except that we're not here for the beaches or wineries or amusement parks," she responded to his comment. "We're here for a family event."

"I like your family," he said.

"You've only met my mother and father." She uncapped her bottle of water—because, of course, she'd packed numerous snacks and drinks for the long trip—and sipped.

"And Diego."

"Who is *not* family."

But he was a close friend who had aspirations of becoming even closer to the family—or at least Alyssa. And he was the reason that Jay had decided to spend the next eight days in California with his temporary girlfriend. "Maybe he's not family, but he'll be at the party, won't he?"

"Considering that he lives in the same neighborhood as my parents, we'll probably cross paths with him frequently over the next week," she acknowledged grimly.

"Then it's a good thing I accepted your mother's invitation, isn't it?" he said.

"I'm not denying that your presence serves a purpose for *me*—I'm just not sure what you're getting out of it."

"The pleasure of your company," he suggested.

She rolled her eyes.

"And, since you mentioned beaches and wineries and amusement parks, maybe we can sneak away for a few hours and do something fun."

"We will," she promised. "I'm just not sure that a few hours of fun will make up for more than a week with my family. And considering how hard it was for me to get someone to cover my shifts at Diggers', I'm wondering how you managed to wrangle ten days off work to make this trip with me."

"I'm the boss," he reminded her.

"Of a business that's been operating for just over a year."

"Operating very successfully," he pointed out. "And one of the reasons it's been so successful is that I hired the right people." A vague memory of Naomi flitted through his mind. "At least when I made my own hiring decisions and didn't let myself be influenced by family pressures."

"Sounds like there's a story there," she noted. "And we've still got about four hours until we get to my parents' place."

So he told her about hiring his cousin, at his father's request—and subsequently firing his cousin, the result of which was that his aunt was still not speaking to her brother, which pleased his mother, who'd never been particularly fond of that sister-in-law.

Alyssa chuckled in all the right places, as if she enjoyed listening to him talk. Over the past few weeks, they'd shared a lot of stories and confidences. As a result, he'd occasionally found himself wondering if this was what it would be like if she was more than just a pretend girlfriend, because being with her had given him an appreciation for what it meant to share a life with someone.

He definitely wasn't in any hurry to get married and start a family, but it was nice to have company at the end of the day, someone to share a meal and conversation.

Over the past several weeks, he'd occasionally wondered what would happen if they moved their relationship to the bedroom, but he never let those thoughts linger. Because wanting anything more than what they had would be selfish and foolish.

And if there was one thing he'd vowed he wouldn't ever be again, it was a fool.

## Chapter Twelve

Alyssa was right—it wouldn't have been difficult for Jay to come up with an excuse as to why he couldn't attend her parents' anniversary party. But when Renata invited him, instead of thinking of reasons why not to make the trip, he'd decided why not make the trip. After all, he enjoyed spending time with Alyssa, and he wasn't ready for this charade to be over.

But what did that mean? Was it possible that he was falling in love with her?

He immediately shrugged off the idea; he wasn't even sure he knew what love was.

Alyssa had the example of her parents to aspire to—Miguel and Renata had been married for thirty-five years and were obviously still in love with one another. The long looks, the subtle touches and shorthand communication all attested to their affection and connection.

His parents didn't demonstrate any of those things.

What they shared, aside from four children, was a love of making money and the status it afforded them in the community. And maybe that was a harsh assessment, but he didn't think it was an inaccurate one. So was it any wonder that he had doubts about his ability to recognize love, if that was what he was feeling?

He'd thought he was in love with Jenny Reashore, the cheerleader he'd dated for several months in high school. In fact, he'd been planning to tell her he loved her after the season opener in his junior year, but that was the night he got sacked and his attention had been diverted by the pain—and then the pain meds they gave him in the hospital. By the time he'd recovered enough to think about sharing his feelings, Jen had already moved on—to Liam Gilmore!—with no more of an explanation than to say "things change."

Yeah, that had cut to the quick. And maybe the experience had made him wary about opening his heart again, but he didn't believe that he'd been scarred so badly that he was incapable of falling in love. In fact, he'd fallen in love with Melanie Lindhurst a few years later, when he was in college. But he'd never said the words to her, either. And when she'd said them to him, he'd started to panic a little, thinking that love meant marriage and kids, and he was barely twenty years old and definitely not ready to make *that* kind of commitment.

But he was twenty-nine now, and he'd noticed that his friends were starting to pair up with their perfect partners. And as he observed their relationships taking shape, he was beginning to see the appeal of sharing his life with someone—especially if that someone was Alyssa.

Or maybe he just needed a strong jolt of caffeine to banish these unexpected thoughts from his mind.

After a quick shower, he followed the scent of coffee into the kitchen, where Alyssa's grandmother was pouring a cup. When he stepped into the room, Valentina reached into the cupboard for a second mug as she slid the first across the counter toward him. "Cream's in the fridge, if you want it. Sugar's on the table."

"This is perfect," he said. "Thanks."

"I usually enjoy my first cup on the deck with the birds for company," she said. "But you're welcome to join us."

"I'd like that," he said, following her through the sliding door and taking a seat across from her.

"Renata will start breakfast as soon as the others get here."

"Others?" he echoed, having visions of the crowd that had gathered the previous evening for a "welcome home" potluck dinner for Alyssa. The group had been comprised of family and friends, including Lucia, Renata's best friend; Daniel, Lucia's husband; and Diego, the favorite nephew. There had been so many people on hand, Jay hadn't been able to pick out Lucia and Daniel, but he noticed that Diego hadn't strayed more than ten feet from Alyssa all night.

Not that she'd seemed aware of or bothered by the other man's presence, but Jay had been both.

"Just Cristina, Steven and Nicolas," Valentina said in response to his question.

"Oh," he said, relieved by the mention of only Alyssa's sister, brother-in-law and nephew.

She smiled as she lifted her mug. "Are you wishing now that you didn't let Alyssa talk you into making this trip with her?"

"Truthfully, she tried to talk me out of it," he confided.

"But you came anyway," she mused.

"I wanted to meet her family." And to remind Diego that Alyssa was with someone else, but he didn't mention that reason to her grandmother.

"Speaking of family," Valentina said, wincing as a car door slammed. "That sounds like Nicolas now."

Not half a minute later, the side gate swung open and the little boy came racing across the grass. "Abuela, hi! Are pancakes ready?"

She rose to her feet and he launched himself at her, wrapping his slender arms around her middle. She stroked an affectionate hand over his hair. "We were waiting for you to get here before we started breakfast."

"I'm here!" he announced.

"I see that."

"And the rest of the neighborhood knows it now, too," Steven said, an obvious commentary on his son's volume.

"You're early," Valentina noted, glancing at the time display on her Fitbit.

"Mom made the mistake of mentioning pancakes to Nicolas last night, and he woke up with them on his mind this morning," Cristina explained.

"It was all we could do to hold him off until eight," her husband confided.

Nicolas looked up at Jay. "D'you like pancakes?"

"I love pancakes," he said.

"Me, too," the boy told him. "Gramma puts 'nanas and choc'late chips in mine sometimes—they're my fav'rite."

"Sounds yummy," he agreed.

"Well, let's go tell your gramma we're here," Cristina suggested, nudging her son toward the house.

Steven went with them.

"And that's the end of our quiet morning," Valentina said with no regret in her tone.

Before Jay could respond, another figure walked through the gate that Alyssa's sister had left open, and his sunny mood turned dark.

"*Buenos días*, Diego."

"*Buenos días*, Abuela," he said, bending down to kiss each of her cheeks. Then he nodded at Jay. "Good morning."

He returned the greeting.

"We're just about to cook up breakfast," Valentina said. "Do you want to join us?"

Jay was glad to see the other man shake his head, declining the offer.

"Thanks, but I ate already. I just stopped by to pick up the casserole dish my mother left last night."

"I'll get it for you," she said.

Nicolas raced out of the house as his great-grandmother was going in. "Bacon's cooking!" he announced. "And Gramma promised to put 'nanas and choc'late chips in my pancakes!" Then he noticed Diego and asked, "Are you going to have breakfast with us?"

This second invitation made it clear to Jay that the other man wasn't just an occasional visitor to the Cabrera house but a frequent guest at their table.

"Not today," Diego responded.

Cristina, never far from her son, set a coloring book and box of crayons on the table, then pulled back a chair for Nicolas to sit.

"Can I help with anything?" Jay asked her, hoping for an excuse to avoid conversation with Alyssa's not-so-secret admirer.

"We've got plenty of hands in the kitchen," Cristina said. "But if you could keep an eye on Nicolas—and keep him out of the kitchen—that would be extremely helpful."

"I can do that," he agreed.

"Thanks," she said, already heading back inside again, leaving Jay alone with her son. And Diego.

The other man didn't waste any time on small talk but bluntly said, "I want you to stop seeing Alyssa."

"I'm sure you do," Jay noted drily.

"She's…fragile," Diego said.

"No, she's not," he argued. "Maybe you want to believe she's fragile so you can tell yourself you're looking out for her, but Alyssa is one of the strongest people I know."

"That doesn't mean she won't be hurt when you toss her aside."

"You're making a lot of assumptions about a relationship—and a man—you know nothing about," he chided.

"Tell me you're serious about wanting a future with Alyssa and I'll back off," Diego said.

"Of course I'm serious about wanting a future with Alyssa," Jay said, and he realized that though he was only repeating the words the other man had told him to say, they weren't untrue.

He did want a future with Alyssa. Maybe he wasn't quite ready to think about putting a ring on her finger, but when he thought about the weeks and even months ahead, he didn't want to imagine his life without Alyssa in it.

The other man scowled. "I don't believe you."

"I don't care what you believe, it's true," he insisted.

"The longer this goes on, the more heartbroken she's going to be when it's over."

"You'd love that, wouldn't you? Because then you could be there to help her pick up the pieces."

"I will be there to help her pick up the pieces," Diego said. "And to show her what it really means to be loved. And when she's ready, I'm going to marry her."

"I hate to destroy this little fantasy world you're building," Jay said, not regretful at all. "But she's not going to marry you."

"How do you know?"

"Because she's going to marry me."

With those words, the arrogant confidence was wiped

from Diego's face. For the first time, the other man looked uncertain. "You didn't... You haven't..."

The stammered response gave Jay a minute to gather his thoughts and correct his course. Because he was clearly on a course that needed correcting.

But Diego's bold assertion had put his back up, and he'd spoken without thinking. Now he had the opportunity to backtrack, at least a little. To suggest that they'd discussed marriage in vague and general terms but eliminate any implication of an actual engagement.

Except that when he opened his mouth to respond, he heard himself say, "Yes, I did. I asked Alyssa to marry me."

"You asked her to marry you?" Diego echoed, his voice hollow.

"And she said yes," he said, because if he ever proposed to a woman, he expected that she would say yes. And because his mouth was apparently a runaway train that his brain didn't know how to stop.

Valentina chose that moment to return with the casserole dish. Diego took it from her with barely a murmured thanks, then left through the side gate again, and Alyssa's grandmother went back inside.

Jay breathed a sigh of relief, confident that he could contain any fallout from that conversation.

Until he remembered the little boy sitting at the table, whose wide eyes confirmed that he'd heard every word.

After the long drive from Nevada and the emotional reunion with her family, Alyssa had fallen into bed exhausted, but sleep had not come easily. And when she'd finally slept, she'd dreamed about Jason.

It was almost seven thirty by the time she dragged herself out of bed. She tied her hair into a ponytail, pulled on a pair of shorts and a T-shirt, laced up her running shoes and slipped out the side door. She'd been tempted to detour downstairs, to see if Jason was up and wanted to go running with her, but she could only imagine how her mother would react if she knew her daughter was knocking on a boy's bedroom door. So she resisted the impulse and headed out on her own.

She did her usual 5K route and returned to the house feeling more like her usual self. After a quick shower and a change of clothes, she was ready to face the day—and her family. Because everyone was gathered around the table for breakfast—not just her parents and grandmother, but her sister, brother-in-law and nephew, too—no doubt lured here by the promise of Renata's pancakes.

"Nicolas just told us the news," Renata said when Alyssa lifted the pot of coffee to fill the mug she'd taken from the cupboard.

She looked from her mother, who was beaming with barely constrained joy, to her nephew, who was busy shoveling pancakes into his mouth, then at the others. Her father nodded, as if in approval, though of what she had no idea; Cristina and Steven were both grinning; Abuela's dark eyes sparkled.

"News?" she echoed blankly.

"He overheard Jason and Diego talking," Valentina said excitedly.

"I can't believe I had to hear it from my grandson." Renata took the lead again. Despite the admonishment of her words, she sounded gleeful rather than disappointed. "Why didn't you tell us last night?"

"Tell you what?" she asked cautiously, lifting her mug to her lips as Jason came in from the deck.

His lips curved when he saw her, but the smile was a little too quick and wide to be natural, and her uneasiness grew.

"That you and Jason are engaged," her mother replied.

Alyssa choked on her coffee.

She looked at Jason, expecting to see the panic that filled her heart reflected in his expression.

Instead, he continued to wear that fake smile as he slid his arm around her and drew her close to his side.

"We didn't say anything because it's still unofficial," he explained. "As you can see, I haven't even had a chance to get a ring yet."

Alyssa didn't know how or why Jason had mentioned marriage. She only knew that she had to rein in the topic before her mother started pressing them to set a date for a wedding that wasn't ever going to happen.

Though her brain was still scrambling to put the pieces together, she felt compelled to say something. "Plus, this week is about celebrating your anniversary," she hastened to add. "And the last thing we'd want to do is steal the spotlight."

"But this is the best news," Renata insisted. "And there is no greater gift to a parent than knowing that her children are loved."

"We should have champagne to celebrate," Miguel decided, obviously caught up in the moment.

"It's 9:30 a.m.," Alyssa pointed out to her father.

"Mimosas, then," Renata said, immediately on board with the plan.

"I'll get the champagne," Steven said, because he knew his in-laws always had a couple chilled bottles in their wine cellar.

"Is that bacon?" Jason asked, eyeing the platter of breakfast meat on the table.

"And sausage and pancakes," Valentina told him. "Come. Eat."

Of course, Jason didn't need to be asked twice.

Alyssa reluctantly joined her "fiancé" at the table, but she only toyed with her food. Even the coffee she'd wanted was now churning uneasily in her tummy. And that was before she had to paste a smile on her face and sip champagne and orange juice as she accepted the best wishes of her family.

After everyone had eaten their fill and the champagne bottle was empty, Alyssa requested a private word with Jason.

She hooked her arm through his and led him outside, all the way to the back of the property, where she could be certain their conversation wouldn't be overheard.

"What was that all about?" she demanded. "Why would you tell my five-year-old nephew that we're getting married?"

"I didn't tell Nicolas anything," he denied.

She dropped her face into her hands. "How— Why—" She drew in a breath and tried again. "How did this happen?"

"He was being a dick."

She frowned. "Nicolas?"

"No," he immediately responded. "Diego."

"I think you need to start at the beginning."

"I was having coffee with your grandmother when he showed up to pick up a dish his mother left here last night.

"Anyway, Valentina went into the house to get it, and as soon as she was out of earshot, Diego confronted me about our relationship. He accused me of playing with your emotions and said that the longer this went on, the more heartbroken you were going to be when it was over, leaving him to pick up the pieces."

"And you responded to that by telling him we're getting married?" she asked incredulously.

He shrugged. "I needed to say something to convince him that he was wrong about our relationship."

"Except that he wasn't," Alyssa reminded him. "Our relationship is a sham."

"I didn't think you wanted me to admit that."

Of course she didn't. But now the lies were getting so much bigger than she'd anticipated, and she felt as if the whole situation was spiraling out of her control.

"Maybe it's time to tell them the truth," she suggested. "We should go back into the house right now and admit that our relationship was a lie from the beginning."

"And then where will I sleep tonight?" he wondered.

She looked at him questioningly. "So what are we going to do?"

"We're going to play this out."

"You can't be serious," she protested.

"If you tell them the truth now, Diego will be back here with a ring before sunset."

"I can handle Diego," she said with more confidence than she felt.

"If you really believed that, our first kiss never would have happened," he pointed out.

"I didn't believe it then," she acknowledged. "But I do now."

"While I appreciate your willingness to blow the cover off our cover story, what purpose would it serve at this point? Besides, it's only for seven days."

"I can't believe you want to maintain the charade of an engagement."

"Pretending to be your fiancé for a week isn't really that much different than pretending to be your boyfriend."

"You don't think so?"

"Only five more days until the big party," Alyssa said to her mother the next morning when she found her in the kitchen, cracking eggs into a bowl for breakfast.

"And we've got a little bit of a problem," Renata said.

"What kind of problem?"

"Tia Deanna and Tio Carlos have decided to come for the celebration. And, of course, they're bringing Selena and Sofia, too."

"Why's that a problem? Aren't you looking forward to seeing them?"

"Of course I am. But we're running out of places to put everybody."

"There are plenty of hotels nearby," she pointed out.

"I can't ask them to stay in a hotel," Renata protested. "They're family."

"So where are they going to sleep?"

"Well, Deanna and Carlos will take the room downstairs, and the girls could squeeze into your room."

"If they're in my room, where am I going to be?"

"In the guest room at Cristina and Steven's place."

"And Jason?" she asked.

"In Nicolas's room."

"Nicolas has bunk beds," she reminded her mother.

Renata nodded. "But the bottom bunk is a double."

With a double-sized comforter that matched the twin— both covered in cartoon dinosaurs. "I assume you've discussed this with Cristina?"

"It was her idea," Renata said.

Alyssa sighed. "I'll tell Jason to pack his bag after breakfast."

"I'm so sorry about this," Alyssa said as Jason drove toward Cristina and Steven's house a few hours later.

"There's no need to apologize," he told her.

"You're going to be sleeping in a bunk bed," she said again in case he hadn't been listening the first two times.

"Which seems to bother you more than it bothers me,"

he pointed out. As long as he had a soft place to lay his head, he wasn't going to complain.

"One dinner a month for the rest of the year."

He turned his head to look at her. "Huh?"

"I owe you big-time for this," she acknowledged. "And a few more home-cooked meals might come close to balancing the scales again."

"Do you have any understanding of how a negotiation works?" he wondered aloud.

"This situation is a lot more than you bargained for," she noted.

"Or maybe you're looking for an excuse to continue spending time with me," he teased.

"You really need to do something about your low self-esteem," she commented wryly.

He shrugged. "I'm not going to turn down your cooking and your company. I was just wondering if there was something more going on here."

"There's nothing more going on here," she assured him. "And now that I think about it, why should I feel responsible for this situation?"

"That's what I'm trying to figure out," he said.

"I'm rescinding my offer," she decided. "Because if this is anyone's fault, it's yours."

"How is this in any way my fault?" he demanded to know.

"If you'd just said that you were busy this week and regretfully unable to attend the party, we wouldn't be in this predicament."

"You're right," he acknowledged. "And you'd be here on your own, free to bask in Diego's attention and affection."

"Okay—the extra dinners are back on the table."

"Well, not yet," he noted. "But I'll count the days."

"You should also hope no one else decides to show up

for this party," she said. "Or we might get bumped out of Cristina and Steven's house, too."

"Welcome to chaos," Cristina said, greeting them from the front porch.

As soon as Alyssa reached the top step, she was folded in her sister's embrace. "I'm so glad you're here." When Cristina released her, Jason was given the same welcome. "And happy to see you again, too."

"Thanks for taking us in," he said.

"Our pleasure," she said, opening the door and gesturing for them to enter. "Steven is in the backyard. He went out to light the grill as soon as Mom called to say you were headed over. Nicolas is with him, because he's been bouncing off the walls all day, eager for 'Tia Lyssa' to arrive.

"Why don't you go out with the men and give Alyssa and me a chance to catch up?" Cristina suggested.

"Sure," he agreed. "Just tell me where to put our bags."

"Oh, just drop them right there for now," Cristina said.

Jason set the bags on the floor as directed.

"I didn't think to ask Alyssa if you were a beer or a wine drinker, but Steven has both outside."

He took the hint and headed toward the doors that were opened onto the back deck.

"I know playing musical beds isn't really convenient, but now we get some one-on-one time without the rest of the family eavesdropping on our conversations."

"You're assuming we have something to talk about that would be worth eavesdropping on," Alyssa said.

"Hello?" Cristina dragged her into the family room and over to the sofa, sitting close to her. "I want the inside scoop on your sexy fiancé."

"What do you want to know?"

"Everything. When? Where? How?" Cristina grinned. "The why is obvious for anyone to see."

Alyssa couldn't blame her sister for having the same visceral reaction most women—including herself—had when they first set eyes on Jason. She just wished Cristina wanted to talk about something, *anything*, other than Alyssa and Jason's phony romance so that she could stop compounding the lies she'd already told her family.

"You know the when, where and how we met," she reminded her sister.

"But not about the engagement."

"Because I didn't want to make a big deal out of it," she said, and that was kind of true, too. Although the bigger truth was that there had been nothing to make a big deal about. "And because nothing is official."

"Maybe you don't have a ring on your finger yet," Cristina said. "But it's obvious that you're both wildly in love."

The only thing obvious to Alyssa was that Cristina wanted to believe her little sister was going to get the happy ending she'd always dreamed of for her. Unwilling to burst her bubble, she only said, "And yet, Diego doesn't see it."

Cristina waved a hand. "Diego doesn't want to see it because he's been in love with you since you were fourteen."

"What are you talking about?"

"The summer Diego's family moved to California, they stayed with Lucia and Daniel while their house was being built," Cristina said.

"I remember that," Alyssa told her.

"Do you remember that Diego had trouble making friends?"

"He was shy."

"So were you," her sister pointed out. "But we were out walking one day, and you saw him dribbling a soccer ball around the yard by himself and invited him to come to Scoops with us."

"You're not honestly suggesting that an ice-cream cone changed his life."

Cristina shrugged. "I've been married for seven years and the male brain is still a mystery to me. But the day after our trip to Scoops, he told me that he was going to marry you."

Alyssa lifted a brow. "He was fifteen. What fifteen-year-old boy talks about marriage?"

"Again—male brain, mystery," her sister said.

"Well, that was twelve years ago," Alyssa pointed out.

"True. But when he saw you again at New Year's, he told me that you were even more beautiful than he remembered and that he was finally going to tell you how he felt about you."

"I didn't even realize he was the same guy," she admitted. "I just knew he was yet another potential future husband Mama was putting in my path."

"She really misses you and wants you to come home," Cristina said.

"She worries about me and doesn't believe I can take care of myself," Alyssa countered.

"That, too," her sister acknowledged. "And I always thought her concern was a little over the top—until Nicolas had to have his tonsils out. A common and minor procedure compared to open-heart surgery, but scary as hell when it's your kid on the operating table."

Alyssa touched a hand to her sister's arm. "I'm sorry I couldn't get back here for that."

"You have your own life to live. And the teddy bear you sent to keep him company in the hospital? He doesn't go to sleep without it."

Alyssa smiled at that. "I wanted him to know I was

thinking about him. And since we're on the subject of Nicolas and sleeping, don't you think it makes more sense for me rather than Jason to bunk with my nephew?"

"Probably," Cristina agreed. "If anybody was going to be bunking with Nicolas."

Alyssa looked at her blankly.

"That's just what I told Mom," her sister explained. "But there's also no way I'd make you or your fiancé sleep in a bunk bed, especially beneath a five-year-old kid who snores worse than Abuela.

"I may be an old married woman now," she continued, "but I remember what it's like to be young and in love." Cristina winked at her. "And recently engaged."

"So where are we going to be sleeping? I mean, where is Jason going to sleep, and where am I?" Alyssa clarified, because the original question sounded as if she expected to sleep *with* Jason.

Her sister's response, "In the guest room," implied the same thing.

And Alyssa realized any hope that a seven-day engagement wouldn't change anything between her and Jason had just taken a major hit.

Because the guest room had only one bed.

## Chapter Thirteen

Jay enjoyed hanging out with Alyssa and her sister and brother-in-law; he was understandably a little wary around her nephew. Aside from the fact that Nicolas had announced the phony engagement to the whole Cabrera family—because apparently telling a five-year-old that something was a secret was a surefire way to get him to shout it out—the little guy did everything at warp speed and full volume. But it was apparent to Jay that the boy adored his Tia Lyssa—and that the feeling was mutual.

For dinner, Steven grilled chorizo sausages that were served with corn on the cob and red rice. The wine and beer flowed freely as the adults enjoyed the warm summer evening, and Nicolas, finally dressed in his pj's with his teeth brushed, climbed into his aunt's lap and fell asleep with his head against her breast.

Watching the boy, Jay experienced an unexpected tug of something he recognized as envy. And how crazy was that—to be jealous of the kid just because he was snuggled close to the soft curves of Alyssa's body?

Yeah, their engagement was a lie. In fact, their whole relationship was a sham. Every part of it, except for his growing attraction to her.

"I should take Nicolas in to his bed," Cristina said, though she didn't look eager to move from the sofa, where she lounged with her head on her husband's shoulder.

"Can I do it?" Alyssa asked.

"Of course," her sister agreed. "Just don't wake him, or he'll be up until midnight."

Alyssa rose easily from her chair with the little boy in her arms.

Jay had observed her interactions with Nicolas for the past several hours. He'd watched her pushing miniature cars around and shooting Nerf darts at a target and using hand puppets to act out a story. In everything she did, she was easy and natural with the boy, and Jay knew she'd be a great mother to her own kids someday.

He got up to open the sliding door for her, and she smiled her thanks as she passed through it.

"Oh, Nicolas dropped Teddy," Cristina said.

"I've got it," Jay said, scooping the stuffed bear from the ground beside the chair where Alyssa had been sitting.

"Thanks," she said. "He doesn't go to sleep without it, and if he wakes up and can't find it, his screams will wake up everyone else, too."

He followed the direction Alyssa had gone and found her tucking the blankets around her nephew in the boy's room.

Jay handed her the bear, and she slipped it under Nicolas's arm.

"I thought I should see where I'm going to be sleeping." He spoke quietly, not wanting to wake the boy.

"Well, you're not sleeping in here," Alyssa responded in a whisper.

"I'm not?"

"No." She kissed Nicolas's cheek, then tiptoed out to the hallway. He followed. "My sister put us in the guest room."

"Guest *rooms*?"

She shook her head. "One room. One bed."

Warning lights flashed in his brain: Danger! Danger!

"You didn't object to that arrangement?" His voice was still low, but there was no mistaking the desperation in his tone.

"What was I supposed to say?" she asked him. "Cristina thinks she's doing us a favor, because what newly engaged couple wouldn't want to snuggle up under the covers?"

Only a short while earlier, he'd been envying Nicolas's proximity to Alyssa, with no expectation that he would soon be getting just as close to her. Closer even. Behind closed doors. Alone.

He swore softly.

She just nodded.

"How big is the bed?"

She led him down the hall to another room, nudged open the door and turned on the light.

"Not big enough," he responded to his own question.

"I'll bet you're wishing now that you'd never offered to make this trip with me," Alyssa remarked.

"Not true," he denied. "Your grandmother's tamales alone were worth the drive."

She smiled at that. "There are moments when I'm really sorry I got you into this mess," she confided. "And other moments when I'm so grateful you were there when Diego walked into Diggers' that night, because I'm not sure Liam would have been such a good sport about this."

"Yeah, that's me—a good sport," he said drily.

"You have been," she insisted.

"It hasn't been without benefits," he reminded her.

"Anything aside from my grandmother's cooking?"

"I would give up her tamales for one of your kisses," he said.

"I saw you chow down on those tamales," she noted.

"They're probably the second best thing I've ever tasted." And though he knew he was playing with fire, Jay pulled her into his arms and kissed her.

And yeah, her mouth was the most delicious thing he'd ever tasted. But instead of satisfying his hunger, he found himself wanting more. Needing more.

His hands slid down her back and over the curve of her bottom, drawing her closer. She lifted her hands to his shoulders, holding on to him as he deepened the kiss. Lips parted, tongues dallied. Desire pulsed through his veins.

A light tap sounded on the partially open door and she practically leaped out of his arms.

"Lys? Are you in there?"

"Yeah." She wrapped her fingers around the knob and yanked the door open wider. "I was just, uh, showing Jason where we were going to be sleeping."

"I didn't mean to interrupt," Cristina apologized, her eyes twinkling. "I just wanted to make sure you have everything you need and to say good-night, because Steven and I are heading to bed, too."

"Oh. Um…yeah. I think we've got everything. Thanks."

"Okay." Cristina kissed her sister's cheek. "Good night." Then, her gaze shifting to Jay, she added, "To both of you."

"Good night," he replied.

"Oh, and lock the door," she advised. "Nicolas is an early riser and he doesn't always remember to knock."

Then she pulled the door firmly closed from the outside, leaving Jay and Alyssa alone.

\* \* \*

They danced around one another as they took turns in the bathroom to get ready for bed.

Alyssa brushed her teeth first, then quickly changed out of her clothes and into her nightshirt while Jason was in the bathroom. When she'd packed for this trip, she'd included her favorite sleeping tee, because she hadn't anticipated that anyone might see her in it. If she had, she might have chosen something that was longer than midthigh—or packed a robe.

Instead, she made do with the covers, ensuring she was under them before he climbed into bed. She lay on her back, her gaze fixed on the ceiling, when he came out of the bathroom. She felt the mattress dip as he lowered himself onto the other side, then he switched off the lamp, plunging the room into darkness.

She shifted, trying to move closer to the edge on her side. But the bed seemed to dip toward the middle, wanting to pull her in the same direction. She shifted again, fighting the worn springs and gravity.

"Could you stop wriggling around for five minutes?" Jason asked through gritted teeth.

"I'm sorry," she said sincerely. "I'm not used to sharing a bed."

"I'm not in the habit of sharing a bed, either. Or not exclusively for sleeping purposes," he clarified.

Which substantiated the rumors that Charming knew how to please a woman, but he didn't do relationships. And even though she was aware of all the reasons it would be a mistake to fall for him, it was getting harder and harder to remember why she shouldn't fall into bed with him. Especially now that they were already there, and her body was intensely aware of his.

"So, how is this going to work?" she asked.

"You're going to close your eyes and go to sleep."

"Oh, okay," she said sarcastically. "Because I haven't tried *that* already."

"Well, try again," he suggested.

So she closed her eyes and imagined that she was alone.

But she could feel the heat of his body and hear the sound of his breathing, and her imagination decided that it preferred to go in a different direction, taunting her with the suggestion of rolling toward him rather than away. Tempting her to imagine those strong, talented hands moving over her body, stripping away her panties and nightshirt, caressing her bare flesh. Touching and teasing and—

Her eyes popped open again in a desperate attempt to banish the fantasy playing out in her mind, making her blood heat and her body yearn. She drew in a slow, deep breath, exhaled.

"I'm used to sleeping in the middle," she confided.

"Me, too," he said. "So obviously that's not going to work for either of us."

Another few minutes passed, the darkness silent and tense, before she ventured to ask, "Do you usually sleep on your back or front or side?"

"How would I know?" he asked her. "I'm sleeping."

The fact that he couldn't see her roll her eyes in the dark didn't stop her from doing it. "What position are you usually in when you wake up?"

That question he answered without hesitation. "Reaching out to silence the damn alarm."

His terse response made her smile, even as she knew it was going to be a very long night.


Alyssa drifted off before he did.

Although sleep didn't come quickly or easily to either of them, Jay sensed the gradual relaxation of her body as her breathing became slow and even. Eventually, his did the same.

He was pretty sure he'd fallen asleep facing the wall, because he remembered deliberately turning onto his side, away from her. Because even when he'd been on his back, with his temporary fiancée on hers, he could see her in his peripheral vision. Even under the covers, he'd been aware of her breasts rising and falling with each breath.

And all he could think about was how perfectly those breasts would fill his hands, how arousing it would be to hear her breath hitch when he brushed his thumbs over her nipples. Even those relatively innocent thoughts had aroused him unbearably, and he'd been grateful she was sleeping, so she couldn't see the sheet tented over a certain part of his anatomy.

But although he was certain he'd fallen asleep facing the wall, he woke up with his arms full of soft, warm female, Alyssa's head tucked under his chin, her hair tickling his throat. He breathed in the scent of her and felt his blood stir.

He loved her softness and her curves. Though he'd heard her grumble about a stubborn seven pounds that refused to be shed, he thought she was perfect.

And right now, her perfect breasts were crushed against his chest. One of her perfect legs was flung over his. And her perfect mouth was only inches from his own.

*Just go with it.*

The four words that she'd spoken to him at Diggers' echoed in his mind. Tempted him.

Of course, she'd been tempting him for weeks now. And the more time he'd spent with her, the harder it had been to resist the temptation—even before he was forced to share a bed with her.

But he was trapped in a web of lies, tangled in so much deceit that he wondered if he'd ever get free. He couldn't blame Alyssa. She'd only wanted a pretend boyfriend for a weekend. He was the one who'd been goaded by his friends to prolong the charade. He was the one who'd raised the stakes of the game—stupidly, perhaps selfishly, but willingly—believing that if Diego couldn't respect that Alyssa had a boyfriend, surely he'd back off in the face of an engagement.

And why did he even care what the other man believed or did? Jay wasn't one of those guys with a hero complex and Alyssa certainly wasn't a damsel in distress. In fact, she was one of the strongest, bravest women he knew. So how had he found himself in this predicament—in bed with a woman who made him ache and whom he didn't dare touch?

He decided it was Gilmore's fault. Though he wouldn't admit as much to Alyssa, her willingness to turn to the other man had been part of his reason for stepping up to the plate. Because he hadn't liked the idea of his sexy neighbor playing out this charade with his high school nemesis—especially considering that he'd lost a girlfriend and his job as starting quarterback to the other man already. So Jay had jumped into this game with no preparation and little hesitation.

Still, he could have backed out at any time before Alyssa's parents made the trip to Haven. And when Renata called, he could have easily made an excuse as to why he couldn't come to California.

Summer was the busiest season at Adventure Village, and everyone else was working extra hours to cover his duties. But he wasn't worried about not being on-site. He trusted Carter to stay on top of everything and to let him know if there were any problems, and his partners were as invested in the success of JC Enterprises as he was.

But the truth was, when Renata mentioned the anniversary celebration, he hadn't been looking for a reason to say no. In fact, he'd been eager to say yes, to have an excuse to spend more time with Alyssa. And *that* was worrisome.

He'd dated a lot of women in his twenty-nine years, although none for any significant period of time. Nat had been right about that. After a few weeks, the shine of any new relationship inevitably began to dull, and he started to withdraw.

He was all about having fun in the here and now, and most of the women he dated wanted the same thing. A couple of his former girlfriends had accused him of being spoiled and selfish, and they probably weren't wrong, but he'd had no desire to change who he was.

Until now.

Until he'd somehow found himself more deeply involved with Alyssa than he'd ever intended.

He hadn't yet decided whether he should blame Nat or thank her—as she insisted he would do—for the situation he found himself in.

His instinct was to pull back from these feelings that were new and unfamiliar, but he didn't want to pull away from Alyssa. Being with her—whether running in the early hours of the morning or sitting under the stars late in the night or anything else at any time in between—just felt right. When he was with her, he wasn't just happy but content, and he couldn't ever recall feeling that way with a woman before. Even after eight weeks of various activities and countless conversations, there was still so much he didn't know about her, so much he wanted to learn.

Was he falling for her? Or had he already fallen?

Was this love?

Or was it just the sexual attraction that simmered between them messing with his head?

Yeah, that made more sense. Because of the terms of their agreement, she was strictly off-limits to him. And forbidden fruit was always the most tempting. So if he wanted to stop fantasizing about getting naked with her, he was going to have to get naked with her.

It made perfect sense to him.

Of course, there was no way it was going to happen in her sister's house. The first time he made love with Alyssa—because his own proximity rules notwithstanding, he no longer doubted that it was going to happen—he wanted to ensure they had complete privacy without the risk of any interruptions.

But damn, it was torture to be so close to her and not be able to touch her the way he wanted to touch her.

Alyssa shifted in her sleep, sighing softly.

Looking up at the ceiling, he silently cursed his friend. Of course, Nat would laugh her ass off if she could see him now, cuddling in bed with a sweet, sexy woman he couldn't allow himself to be intimate with. Not here. Not now.

And not for any of the five more nights he'd be sleeping with Alyssa in this bed.

He almost wished he'd been assigned to the bottom bunk in her nephew's room. Or the sofa in the living room. Hell, even the floor of the garage would be easier than this.

"You're killing me, Lys."

His words, muttered through gritted teeth, failed to penetrate the cloud of slumber that continued to envelop her, because she only snuggled closer.

Her breasts rubbed against his chest, the friction causing her nipples to pebble beneath the soft cotton of her nightshirt. A shirt that had ridden up during the night, so that her legs and the sweet curve of her bottom—barely covered by silky panties—were exposed.

Thankfully, he'd had the forethought to bring a pair of pajama pants and a T-shirt. At home, he slept only in his briefs, but he didn't think that was the best choice for her parents' house. Sharing a bed with Alyssa, he was doubly grateful for the extra clothing barrier between them.

"Lys?" He tried again.

"Mmm." Her eyelids fluttered open. "Oh." Her sleepy eyes widened. "Um…"

"I guess we both ended up sleeping in the middle, after all," he said when she didn't seem able to complete her thought.

"I guess we did," she acknowledged, her cheeks flushing prettily.

She eased back and attempted to extricate her limbs from his. Her thigh grazed the front of his pants and her breath caught.

"You're…um…" Her words trailed off again.

"Aroused?" he suggested drily.

She nodded, the color in her cheeks deepening.

"That's what happens when a guy wakes up with a sexy, half-naked woman sprawled over him."

She quickly shifted farther away. "I'm so sorry," she said. "I'm not used to…um…"

"You don't have to apologize," he told her. "But it would be helpful if you didn't cuddle me like Nicolas's teddy bear for the next few nights."

"Five more nights," she reminded him.

He nodded, painfully aware of the time frame. "Let's just try to get through one day—and night—at a time," he suggested.

She sighed. "This whole thing has gotten so complicated."

"On the plus side, I think your parents are starting to like me."

"My parents *do* like you," she confirmed. "My grandmother described you as very hot, Tia Deanna used words that made me blush and my sister and cousins all think you're incredibly handsome and charming."

"So why don't you sound happy?" he asked her.

"Because I didn't expect them to like you quite so

much," she admitted. "They're all going to be so disappointed when we call off our engagement."

He lifted a hand to brush her hair away from her face. "I really put my foot in it, didn't I?"

"I appreciate what you were trying to do," she said. "And truthfully, it's not just about the engagement. They'd be equally disappointed to hear about our breakup even if they never thought we were planning to get married, so I guess it's really my fault for coming up with the pretend boyfriend idea in the first place."

"At this point, instead of assigning blame, we should focus on getting through the rest of this trip without crossing that line we said we weren't going to cross. Unless—" his tone turned hopeful as another thought crossed his mind "—you want to renegotiate the terms of this agreement."

"Or we could say there's been some kind of crisis at Adventure Village and you have to go back," she suggested as an alternative.

"What kind of crisis would make me abandon my fiancée at her parents' thirty-fifth anniversary celebration?" he asked. "Because I don't think a shortage of paintballs or a malfunctioning laser vest would suffice."

"Maybe a family emergency," she began, then immediately shook her head, horrified by the words she'd spoken. "Ohmygod, no. I didn't mean— I can't believe that thought even came into my head. And I didn't mean a *real* emergency, just that you could make something up."

"Isn't making things up what got us into this situation in the first place?" he asked her.

She sighed again. "You're right. I just wanted to get you out of this increasingly awkward situation."

"I'm not going anywhere. Except—" he pushed back the covers and climbed out of bed "—to take a very cold shower."

## Chapter Fourteen

Though much of Alyssa and Jason's time was spent with her family, helping to prepare for the big anniversary celebration that was the purpose of their trip, she was pleased that they'd managed to slip away on a few occasions so that she could show her seven-day fiancé some of the local sights.

They'd toured a Southern California winery, visited a local art gallery and even spent a whole day with Nicolas. Alyssa told Jason that she wanted to give Cristina and Steven some time to themselves—which was true, but he quickly figured out that her nephew was her excuse to make a trip to Disneyland.

Today she'd brought Jason to Laguna Beach so they could watch the sunset from the sandy shores. As they walked hand in hand on the beach, she found herself reflecting on the time she'd spent with him over the past several weeks and everything she'd learned about him.

He was thoughtful and kind and surprisingly sweet.

Yeah, he had a bit of a sarcastic edge, and an unreasonable aversion to green vegetables, but in so many other ways, he was practically perfect.

So how was it that no woman had snapped him up?

Of course, she knew the answer to that question: he wouldn't let himself be snapped up.

He was the perfect boyfriend in the moment, because that was all he wanted. Maybe he'd done a good job playing "family man" with Nicolas, but that was only for a day, and she knew better than to let her mind wander too far down that path. Thinking about long-term plans with Jason would be a heartbreak waiting to happen.

Still, she found herself wondering. "Have you ever had a serious girlfriend?"

"That's a strange question for a woman to ask her fiancé," he noted.

"Fake fiancé," she clarified. "And I'd argue that it's the kind of information a woman should know about the man she's pretending she wants to marry."

"Sure, I had a couple of serious girlfriends in the past." He slid an arm across her shoulders. "But only one fiancée."

She rolled her eyes. "I'm trying to have a real conversation with you."

"Am I preventing that in some way?"

She ignored his question to ask another one of her own. "Have you ever been in love? And telling a woman you love her for the purpose of getting her naked doesn't count."

"I've never had to lie to a woman to get her naked."

She had no doubt *that* was true. All he had to do was look at her and she got so hot, she was ready to strip down for him. "That doesn't answer my question."

"Personally, I think people put too much stock in the word *love*," he said.

"And I think you're avoiding the question," she countered. "But I'll rephrase it—have you ever been in a relationship with someone you thought you would spend the rest of your life with?"

"No. Maybe." He reconsidered, then shook his head. "No."

"Tell me about the maybe," she urged.

"Melanie Lindhurst. I met her in college. We were together for a few months, and there was a brief moment when I imagined she was the one."

"What happened?"

"I realized that being with one person for the rest of my life meant never being with anyone else and decided that wasn't for me."

She immediately shook her head. "There's got to be more to the story."

"I was twenty years old, and there were more hot women on the Berkeley campus than the entire population of Haven. I wasn't ready to limit my options."

"I agree that twenty is young to be thinking about 'ever after,'" she said. "But I also know that you're not nearly as shallow as you pretend to be."

He scoffed at the idea. "Why would I pretend to be shallow?"

"Maybe to ensure that no one expects too much from you," she suggested.

He was quiet for several minutes before he finally responded. "Melanie liked to talk about the future, weeks or even months and years down the road, as if it was a given that we'd be together. And I didn't have the same faith that everything would work out the way she wanted it to."

"Why not?" Alyssa asked gently.

"You've met my parents," he reminded her. "They're hardly an example of wedded bliss."

"You don't think they're happy together?"

"Their marriage just seems a little…hollow," he decided. "And definitely not something I want to emulate."

"Every relationship is different."

"I get that now, but I had a limited frame of reference back then, and when Melanie told me she loved me—I panicked."

"Do you ever think back and wish you hadn't panicked?" she asked him.

"No."

"Then maybe you didn't love her," she suggested.

"Maybe I didn't, but it felt real at the time."

His admission made Alyssa feel better about her growing feelings for him. The more time she spent with Jason, the more she liked him. Despite his reputation as a ladies' man, he was attentive and thoughtful and his kisses…

Just the memory of those kisses was enough to make her knees weak.

But what he said made perfect sense. Since they'd embarked on this trip to California, they'd barely been apart from one another. It was understandable that the physical proximity would intensify her feelings for him. No doubt her emotions only seemed so huge and real right now because of the situation they found themselves in.

But she was optimistic that, when they went back to Haven and their normal routines, those feelings would fade. And in the future, after she'd fallen truly and deeply in love, she would no doubt look back on this moment and acknowledge that "it felt real at the time" but was, by then, just a pleasant memory.

The day of the anniversary celebration, Jason was recruited by the men to help set up the tent and chairs in the backyard, so he went over to Renata and Miguel's house with Steven, while Alyssa and Cristina stayed back with Nicolas to get ready for the party.

Alyssa had packed her favorite little black dress for the occasion. It was a sleeveless halter style chiffon with a cascading panel that made her feel feminine and sexy. She paired it with high-heeled black sandals that added three inches to her height and finished the look with crystal teardrop earrings.

When she'd finished pinning up her hair and had added a light touch of makeup, she decided to see if her nephew wanted to play Go Fish before they had to leave for the party. She found him in the kitchen snacking on one of the cupcakes his mom had made for the dessert table. He jumped down from his booster seat when he saw "Tia Lyssa" and ran to hug her.

"Nicolas, no!" his mother said.

But she was too late.

The little boy had already pressed his face—smeared with white icing—against the front of Alyssa's black dress.

"Oh, no," Cristina said when she saw the unmistakable evidence of her son's affection on her sister's skirt.

Nicolas wasn't quite sure what he'd done wrong, but his big brown eyes grew even bigger as they filled with tears.

"It's okay," Alyssa said, wanting to reassure both of them. "I'm sure it'll wipe off."

But it didn't. In fact, dabbing at the white streaks only made more of a mess.

"I'll pay to have it cleaned," Cristina immediately offered.

"That's not necessary," Alyssa said.

Because they both knew the cost of cleaning the dress wasn't the issue—it was that there was no way it could be cleaned before the party.

"Okay, let me get Nicolas washed up, then I'll see what I can find in my closet for you to wear."

A few minutes later, Cristina entered the guest room with an armload of dresses.

"I only need one," Alyssa couldn't resist teasing.

"But we need to figure out which one is the best one," her sister said.

"Anything that fits is fine."

Cristina shook her head. "You never did like to play dress-up, did you?"

"And you always loved to put on fancy clothes and shoes and paint your face with Mama's makeup," she remembered.

"Good times," her sister agreed with a smile. "Having you here reminds me of those times."

"It has been fun."

"Aside from my son destroying your dress, you mean?"

"Nicolas didn't destroy anything," Alyssa assured her.

"Can you tell how much he's missed you?"

"Not half as much as I've missed him. And you."

"I've missed you, too," Cristina said. "But I can see that living in Nevada has been good for you. Or maybe it's Jason Channing who's been good for you."

Alyssa managed a smile, ignoring the twinge of guilt that jabbed in her belly because she was lying to her sister.

Cristina had always been the one person she could be completely honest with. When she'd been frustrated by endless medical appointments and the limitations her parents put on her activities, her sister was the one she'd talked to. Cristina had listened with understanding and without judgment, and she'd offered encouragement when Alyssa started running. In fact, Cristina seemed to understand—maybe even better than Alyssa did herself—that running was a way of proving that she was in charge of not just her body but her life.

But if Alyssa told her the truth about her relationship with Jason now, Cristina would be appalled to realize that she'd made her little sister share a bed with a man who not only wasn't her fiancé but not even a real boyfriend.

"What about this one?" Cristina asked, holding up a sheath-style dress.

"It's red."

"And?"

"I don't wear red."

"Why not? This would look fabulous on you."

Alyssa eyed the slim jersey knit. "I doubt I could even squeeze into it."

"Give it a try," Cristina implored.

So Alyssa took off her icing-smeared garment and tugged her sister's dress over her head.

"Well," Cristina said, "I don't think I'm ever going to be able to wear that again."

"Am I stretching it out?" Alyssa reached for the hem to pull it off again.

"No." Her sister touched her arm, halting her actions. "Because it looks a lot better on you than it does on me."

Alyssa chewed on her lower lip as she looked at her reflection in the mirror. "I think I should try the gray one."

Cristina shook her head. "No," she said again. "I'm not letting you hide in the background."

"Mom's eyes will pop out of her head when she sees me in this dress."

"Probably," her sister acknowledged, a slow smile curving her lips. "But so will Jason's."

Alyssa picked up her necklace, fastened it around her throat.

"I can't believe you still wear that," Cristina said.

"Why not?"

"It was kind of a tongue-in-cheek gift," her sister said.

"It's a beautiful necklace."

"I wouldn't have bought it if I didn't think so, but I didn't intend for you to use it as a shield."

"What are you talking about?"

"Honey, the necklace does absolutely nothing for that dress. The only purpose it serves is to cover up the part of your barely visible scar that peeks over the top of the dress."

"You know how Mama is about my scars," Alyssa said.

"I do know," Cristina agreed. "But that's her problem, not yours."

"Jason once said almost the exact same words."

"Obviously your fiancé is a very wise man."

He *was* wise, but he wasn't really her fiancé.

But, of course, she didn't say that to her sister.

Jay could understand why it was so hard for Alyssa to deceive her family about their relationship. The Cabreras were genuinely warm and welcoming people, and the more time he spent with Renata and Miguel—and especially Valentina—the more uneasy he felt about the lies.

If and when he got married and had a family, he hoped—

*Whoa!* He severed that thought as soon as it began to form.

Marriage?

Family?

Neither of those ideas should be anywhere on his radar. Not right now, anyway. He was only twenty-nine years old and the CEO of a young start-up company. He had no business—and no desire—to be thinking about long-term plans.

So why couldn't he stop thinking about Alyssa?

It was a question that nagged at him throughout the day.

And when he returned to Cristina and Steven's house with Alyssa's brother-in-law, he wasn't any closer to an answer.

He stripped down for a quick shower and thought about the fact that they'd been together almost constantly since they'd embarked on this road trip. That was undoubtedly the reason she'd been on his mind so constantly. As soon as they got back to Haven and got some distance, he was confident that everything would go back to normal. Alyssa would be his date for Matt's wedding, but nothing more.

His conviction lasted only until she walked into the room.

"You look…wow."

Her smile was a little uncertain. "Is it too much?" She glanced down. "Or too little?"

"I'd say it's just right."

"It's not the dress I'd planned to wear," she told him. "But there was a little mishap in the kitchen, so I had to raid Cristina's closet."

"It's lucky you wear the same size."

"We don't really," she said. "I would have bought this dress one size bigger—or probably not at all."

"It's perfect," he insisted. "Although I would like to make one suggestion."

"What's that?"

"Lose the necklace."

Her hand immediately went to the misshapen heart dangling at the end of the chunky chain around her neck. "What? Why?"

"Because it takes away from the neckline of the dress."

"Now you're a stylist?" she challenged.

"I'm gonna say no to that, because I'm not sure I even know what a stylist is," he said. "But I am a man who appreciates the attributes of a woman."

"I like the necklace," she insisted.

"You like hiding your scars," he said.

"So?"

"So you're a strong, brave, beautiful woman and your scars don't in any way take away from that."

"Yeah, I heard that surgical incisions are surpassing tattoos and piercings as the new body art," she said sardonically.

"Maybe they're not art," he acknowledged. "But they're not flaws or imperfections, either. Why can't you see them as badges of courage?"

"Because I didn't do anything courageous. I just happened to be born with a defective heart that the doctors fixed for me."

"You survived," he reminded her. "And the world is a much better place with you in it."

"That was kind of cheesy," she told him.

"But kind of sweet, too?" he prompted.

She managed a smile. "Yeah."

She slowly turned to face the mirror, then took a deep breath and reached for the heart. Her fingers trembled as she worked the toggle through the hole, then pulled the necklace away and set it on top of the dresser.

He put his hands on her shoulders and let his eyes skim over her reflection in the mirror. "Wow," he said again, softly, reverently.

She lifted a hand, subconsciously rubbing the top of the scar, visible above the square neckline of her borrowed dress.

He caught her wrist and pulled her hand away.

"Look at yourself," he said. "You're beautiful, Alyssa. Absolutely breathtakingly beautiful."

"When you look at me like that, I feel beautiful," she admitted.

"Then I will spend the whole night looking at you," he promised.

"I like the sound of that," she agreed. "But maybe you could focus on the road while you're driving?"

"All right," he agreed. "But only while I'm driving."

When they got to Renata and Miguel's house, Nicolas led the way, as comfortable at his grandparents' home as he was at his own. Cristina and Steven followed their son, with Alyssa and Jason trailing behind them.

As usual, most of the activity was happening in the kitchen, where the food was going to be laid out, buffet style, for the guests to help themselves. Alyssa set the black bean salad on the table, where her mother was fussing over an arrangement of flowers.

Renata greeted each of the new arrivals, then said to Alyssa, "Is that Cristina's dress?"

Valentina, who was sprinkling grated cheese on top of a tray of enchiladas that were ready to go in the oven, glanced over.

"It is," Alyssa confirmed.

"But it looks better on Lys than it ever did on me," Cristina said as she put the tray of cupcakes on top of the fridge, safely out of reach of eager little hands.

"I have a silk scarf that I picked up in Florence last summer with touches of that same color," her mother said.

"It's too warm for a scarf," Abuela interjected, dismissing the suggestion.

"It's a decorative accessory that would look great with the dress," Renata insisted. "Why don't we go take a look?"

"Actually—" Jason surprised everyone by speaking up "—I think Alyssa looks perfect just as she is."

Her mother's cheeks flushed. "She does, of course," she agreed. "I just thought the dress could use a little…pop."

"I'd say her curves add enough pop," Valentina said, winking at Alyssa.

"Thanks, Abuela," she said. "Because I wasn't already feeling self-conscious enough."

"A woman should never be self-conscious about her attributes," her grandmother said, looking pointedly at Renata.

Steven clapped a hand on Jason's shoulder. "I think this would be a good time for us to make sure the bar's stocked."

"An important task," Jason agreed, although he looked to Alyssa as if to ensure that she didn't mind him sneaking away from the increasingly awkward conversation.

She gave a quick nod, and the two men made their escape.

"I don't like seeing your scars," Renata admitted. "Because they're a reminder of the scariest time in my life, when I thought I might lose my precious baby girl."

Alyssa took her hands. "The last surgery was more than twenty years ago, Mama."

Her mother sniffled, nodded. "I know. But that doesn't always seem like so very long ago."

"Why don't you show me the scarf?" she suggested.

But Renata shook her head. "Your Jason is right—you look wonderful just as you are."

Alyssa didn't feel wonderful—she felt like a fraud. Because Jason wasn't "hers" and nothing about their relationship was real. But as much as she wished she could dispense with the deception, she'd taken it too far to turn back now.

"You're so much stronger than I ever gave you credit for being," Renata said to her now. "I'm glad you've finally found a man who recognizes and appreciates not just your strengths but many other wonderful qualities."

"Well, he appreciates my cooking, anyway," Alyssa said lightly.

"I guess I'm going to have to tell Lucia that our hopes of a romance blossoming between my youngest daughter and her favorite nephew were for naught."

"I didn't realize she was complicit in your plan."

"All we did was put the two of you together, hoping you would connect," Renata said. "And I didn't do it because I didn't think you could find a wonderful man on your own, but because I hoped falling in love with someone here would give you incentive to move back home."

"I miss you, too," Alyssa told her mother. "But I have a good job and good friends in Haven—a good life."

"And Jason."

"Of course," she said quickly, because any woman would surely put her fiancé at the top of her list.

"But you'll get married here, won't you?"

The question reinforced the necessity of telling her mother the truth sooner rather than later—she couldn't let Renata continue to dream about a wedding that wasn't going to happen. But for now she only said, "Yes, Mama. When I'm—*we're*—ready to get married, it will be here, and I'll wear Abuela's wedding gown, like I always planned."

Her mother's eyes misted as she pictured the scene Alyssa described.

"But today is about celebrating *your* wedding," she reminded Renata, guiding her outside so the celebrations could begin.

And so her lies could stop—at least for a little while.

## Chapter Fifteen

Alyssa had a lot of reasons for moving to Haven, one of which was to escape the constant comparisons to her sister. By the time Cristina was twenty-six, she'd been married for four years and had a two-year-old child. Alyssa had simpler dreams, at least in the short-term—and she needed some time to figure out what she wanted for her own life before she could share it with someone else.

And yet, celebrating her parents' thirty-fifth anniversary, watching them interact together and listening to their stories, she could see the benefits of having a partner to share the good times and the bad. Someone to laugh with and lean on, to plan with and care for. Growing up, she'd taken so much for granted. She hadn't appreciated the special closeness her family shared until she'd moved away. And while she wasn't necessarily in any hurry to walk down the aisle, she knew now that she did want what her parents had and what Cristina had found with Steven.

"Everything okay, honey bear?" Jason asked, returning from the bar with a glass of wine for Alyssa.

"Aside from you calling me 'honey bear,' yeah," she said and offered him a smile in exchange for the wine. "I was just counting my blessings."

"You are a lucky woman," he agreed. "You have a wonderful family, good friends and a handsome and adoring fiancé whose mother made him take dance lessons as a kid."

"Really?"

He offered his hand. "Shall I prove it to you?"

She set her glass of wine on the table. "Show me what you've got."

Though his brain had cautioned him to avoid close physical contact, Jay knew there was no way to maintain the illusion of their relationship without a few turns around the dance floor. And after sleeping in the same bed for the past five nights, he didn't think a dance was anything he couldn't handle.

But the music was soft and seductive, and she fit perfectly in his arms, almost as if she was meant to be there. Dancing with Alyssa, he felt as if everything he'd ever wanted was literally within his grasp.

He immediately chided himself for the ridiculous notion, but the idea continued to nudge not just at his mind but his heart.

"Who's that in the flowered dress?" he asked, turning Alyssa around so she could see the woman in question.

"That would be Lucia."

"Diego's aunt," he said, connecting the dots. "Now I know why she's been shooting daggers at me with her eyes."

"Didn't you meet her at the potluck?"

"I missed that pleasure," he said drily.

"Well, she was extremely disappointed—my mother's words—to learn that I was planning to marry someone other than her favorite nephew."

"So maybe you are glad that I'm here," he suggested.

She tipped her head back to smile at him. "There's no *maybe* about it. I *am* glad you're here."

"Then let's make sure Lucia knows it," he said and lowered his mouth to hers.

Of course, the moment their lips touched, he forgot about Lucia and Diego and the hundred-plus other guests. In that moment, there was only Alyssa, and he'd never wanted anyone more.

Maybe their relationship had started as "plan B," but over the past few weeks, everything had changed. *He* had changed. And the feelings that filled his heart when he was with her were deeper than anything he'd ever felt before.

Their reasons for agreeing to this charade were in the past. Now he was focused on the present—and looking to his future with Alyssa.

They were up early the next morning to head back to her parents' house for an early breakfast before they started the return trip to Nevada. Alyssa had enjoyed visiting with her family and she knew she'd miss them like crazy when she was gone, but she was also looking forward to returning to Haven and the life she'd built for herself there. Over the past week, Jason had played the part of the doting fiancé almost too well, convincing Renata and Miguel that he was in love with their youngest daughter and looking forward to planning a life with her. While she appreciated his efforts, that was an illusion she needed to dispel before she started to believe it.

When breakfast was over, Alyssa steered her mother away from the gathering for a private word.

"I need to tell you something before I go," she began.

Renata's brow furrowed, a familiar sign of concern. "You're not pregnant, are you?"

Alyssa felt her cheeks burn as she shook her head. "No, I'm not pregnant. I'm also not engaged to Jason."

Her mother's eyes grew wide. "You turned down his proposal?"

"No, Mama. He never really asked me to marry him."

"I don't understand."

"We've only been dating a few months," she said, because although she couldn't continue the deception of the engagement, she wasn't ready to admit that their whole relationship had been a lie from the beginning. "And although we enjoy one another's company, it's far too soon to be thinking of a lifetime together."

"Then why did he tell Diego that you'd agreed to marry him?" Renata wondered aloud.

"Because Diego didn't seem to care that I had a boyfriend and Jason hoped he'd back off if he believed our relationship was more serious than it is," she explained.

"Diego has been rather…persistent," her mother admitted. "And perhaps that's my fault. I did encourage him to pursue you—and to not give up. But all that was before we met Jason. Before we knew you were in love."

"I don't blame you, Mama," Alyssa said. "But there's also no reason to tell Diego—or Lucia—that the engagement isn't real."

"And maybe it will be…someday."

"Maybe," she agreed, unwilling to completely destroy her mother's hopes. "But that potential someday is far off."

"Maybe not as far as you think," Renata said. "In the meantime, it's comforting to know that you have such a fine young man looking after you in Haven."

"I can look after myself, Mama."

"Well, of course you can." Her mother's immediate agreement was a surprise. "But there's nothing wrong with letting someone take care of you every once in a while, as I'm sure you take care of him, too."

Alyssa hadn't thought too much about the give and take in a romantic relationship, because she'd never really been in one before. Of course, she wasn't in one now, either, but being a counterfeit couple had given her a taste of the kind of sharing that came with being in a real relationship. She enjoyed listening to Jason talk about his stresses and worries and hearing funny stories about things that happened during his day. And she realized that being taken care of by a man didn't need to be a negative thing, so long as she was taking care of him, too.

Of course, that man wouldn't ever be Jason Channing, because he'd been clear from the beginning that their bogus romance would never lead to anything real.

Returning to Haven, where he had a king-size mattress to himself, Jay thought he would finally be able to sleep. But when he crawled beneath the covers that first night back, his bed felt big and empty without Alyssa. He missed the scent of her skin, the warmth of her body and just knowing that she was beside him.

And when he finally did sleep, he dreamed about her.

He skipped his run the next morning. Though he'd been anxious to get home and back to what was familiar, he needed some distance from Alyssa, space to clear his head of the ridiculous thoughts that had taken root when they were together in California and purge his heart of the unwelcome feelings that had started to root within. Except that not being with her didn't stop him from thinking about her. Missing her. Wanting her.

He wasn't used to a woman featuring so prominently

in his thoughts. As a result, he was distracted and short-tempered at work, like an addict going cold turkey in a desperate attempt to break his habit. And it didn't work. Despite his concerted efforts not to think about her, he couldn't think about anything else.

He went running that night, determined to establish a new routine for himself—a routine that didn't include Alyssa. But damn, he missed her presence beside him.

He didn't run Tuesday morning, either, because he'd done ten miles the night before. Then he skipped Wednesday, too—opting to go into work early and stay late. And all day, she was on his mind.

When he got home, he surveyed the meager contents of his fridge in search of something to eat. He was trying to determine the age of some frozen leftover pizza when there was a knock on the door.

His heart knocked against his ribs, anticipating who might be on the other side. And again when he opened the door and found Alyssa standing there.

"I should have called," she said. "But I thought it might be better to have this conversation face-to-face."

"That sounds ominous," he noted.

She shook her head. "It's not. I just wanted to let you know that it's okay if you've changed your mind about me being your date on the fourteenth, because I can pick up an extra shift at—"

"Whoa!" He held up a hand. "Are you trying to renege on our deal?"

"No," she denied. "I'm letting you off the hook."

He pulled the door open wider and gestured for her to enter. "Maybe you should come inside for this conversation."

She hesitated, no doubt wondering why he was suddenly so eager for her company, but finally accepted his invitation.

"Do you want a glass of wine?" he offered.

"Okay," she said. "That would be nice."

He didn't think about the fact that he'd started to stock her favorite brand—he just uncorked one of the bottles and poured a glass for her, then another for himself.

"Now tell me why you think I want to be let off a hook I didn't even know I was on," he suggested when he'd taken a seat beside her at the island.

"Because you've been avoiding me since we got back from California."

"I haven't been avoiding you," he denied.

She shook her head. "We've told a lot of lies to other people," she acknowledged. "But I thought we were at least honest with one another."

"I've had a lot of work to catch up on, so I've been heading in early," he told her.

"I guess that's what happens when you take a week away during your busiest season," she remarked.

"It was my choice to go," he reminded her.

"And now you regret it."

Maybe he did, but not for reasons that had anything to do with his business. "No," he said. "I had a great time with you."

And he'd gotten so used to being with her 24/7, he'd started to feel as if something was missing when he wasn't with her. That was why he'd deliberately attempted to put some distance between them—to prove that he could. To prove to himself that he wasn't falling for her.

So far, he remained unconvinced. And the way his heart bounced around inside his chest whenever he saw her suggested something completely different.

"But now you're trying to put as much distance as possible between us," she accused. "Because the pretend dating thing started to feel a little too real."

"Maybe it did start to feel real," he acknowledged. "Or maybe it *got* real."

Her brows drew together as she considered that. "I don't want to lose your friendship, Jason."

"You're not going to."

"Okay," she said. "But if you've changed your mind about your friend's wedding—"

"I haven't changed my mind." And even if he had, his agreement with Kevin prevented him from amending their plans. "I'll pick you up at three o'clock on Saturday."

She finished her wine and set down the empty glass. "I'll be ready."

"One more thing," he said as she pushed away from the counter.

"What's that?"

"Wear something red."

She seemed surprised by the request. "There's a color scheme for the wedding guests?"

"No," he said. "You just look really good in red."

And he was clearly an infatuated fool, because after promising himself that he would put some distance between them, his resolve had crumbled in less than three days. And he was already counting the hours until Saturday, when he would see her again.

Alyssa was accustomed to dressing in subtle colors and modest styles; she didn't own a red dress and had no intention of buying one.

Until she remembered the way Jason had looked at her when she'd been wearing the scarlet-colored sheath borrowed from her sister's closet. She wanted him to look at her like that again.

She wanted him to want her as much as she wanted him.

They'd agreed that their fake relationship would end

after the wedding, but Alyssa hadn't given up hope that she might experience real passion with Jason. But first she had to convince him to break through the boundaries he'd established for their relationship, and she didn't have the first clue how to do that.

Thankfully, she did know someone who was something of an expert on human behavior. So she invited Skylar to go shopping with her to find something appropriate for the wedding, and because she hoped her friend might be able to give her some much-needed advice on how to seduce a man who'd made it clear he would not be seduced.

"When's the wedding?" Sky asked as she looked through a rack of dresses at the upscale boutique in Battle Mountain that she'd declared was the only place to shop within driving distance of Haven.

"Saturday," Alyssa confided.

"Matt Hutchinson and Carrie Morgan's wedding?"

"You know them?"

Her friend nodded. "I went to school with Carrie's sister, Courtney. And Liam actually dated Carrie a few years back. In fact, you'll probably see him at the wedding."

"Is he taking a date?" Alyssa asked.

"Heather," Sky admitted with a roll of her eyes.

"They're back on again?"

"He says no, but going to a wedding together says something else," her friend noted.

"Why is the event significant?" Alyssa wondered.

"Because weddings tend to make people reflect on their own lives—where they are and what they want. And when they realize they haven't accomplished everything they'd hoped to, they turn to alcohol and sex to feel better about themselves."

"Is this something you've researched?" Alyssa asked.

"Not specifically," Sky said. "But I've been to a lot of weddings."

She considered her friend's revelation. "Are you suggesting that guys who've reached their goals are less interested in post-wedding sex?"

"Oh, no. They want to get laid, too," Sky assured her. "But their rationale is that they've earned it."

Alyssa laughed at that.

But a long time later, after they'd finished shopping, she ventured to ask, "What do you think it means when a guy doesn't want to have sex?"

"Is there such a creature?"

"Apparently."

Her friend's gaze narrowed thoughtfully. "Are you telling me that you and Jason haven't done the deed?"

Alyssa almost wished she hadn't said anything, but there wasn't anyone else she could talk to about the subject, so she nodded in response to the question.

"I'm sure I'm not telling tales out of school by saying that your boyfriend has a bit of a reputation as a ladies' man, so to discover that he hasn't taken you to bed is more than a little surprising."

"But we're only fake dating," she reminded her friend.

"And how long has this been going on?"

"Well, if anyone asks, the story is six months. But we've only been real fake dating for three, because that started on what was supposedly our three-month anniversary."

Sky shook her head. "Real fake dating? Are you hearing yourself?"

"I know it sounds crazy," she acknowledged.

"Admitting you have a problem is the first step on the road to recovery," Sky said. "But I'm curious…during this period of fake dating, have you been fake holding hands and fake kissing, too?"

"Yes, because those public displays are a necessary part of the illusion."

"So he's never touched you behind closed doors? Never kissed you good-night when no one was watching?"

"Occasionally," she admitted.

"But he hasn't tried to get you naked?" Sky pressed.

Alyssa shook her head. "I've been waiting—and hoping—for him to make a move, but…nothing."

"So make the move yourself," her friend advised.

"You make it sound so easy."

"Men really aren't complicated creatures."

"Maybe he hasn't made a move because he's not attracted to me," Alyssa suggested.

Her friend immediately shook her head. "I've seen the way he looks at you—he's definitely attracted."

She crossed her fingers that Sky was right. Because if she didn't succeed in making a move Saturday night—or inspiring Jason to make a move—her window of opportunity would be closed forever.

"Well, now that I've got the dress, shoes and earrings, can we finally go for lunch?"

"Just one more quick stop," Sky said.

"It better be quick—I'm starving."

Her friend paused outside The Grill. "You go in and get a table. I'll be back in five."

So Alyssa did.

Five minutes later, her friend came into the restaurant and dropped a paper bag in her lap.

"What's this?" Alyssa asked.

"What all the cool kids are wearing," Sky told her.

She put down her menu and peeked in the bag. Apparently the cool kids were wearing America's #1 Condom. "I wish I had half your faith that I'm going to need these."

"Honey, I've seen you in that dress. You don't need

faith—but you need to be smart. Of course, some might argue that wanting to get naked with Jason Channing isn't smart," she said, because apparently a Gilmore couldn't resist taking a dig at a Blake any more than a Blake could at a Gilmore. "But since you've set your sights in his direction, you should be prepared."

When Alyssa responded to Jay's knock on her door, the first thing he noticed was that she'd complied with his request. The second was that his efforts to put distance between them had done nothing to lessen his attraction to her. Because all it took was one look—that first look—and the desire he'd been trying to deny surged through his veins.

The neckline of the dress was high enough to ensure that her scars weren't visible, but the back dipped low, revealing lots of smooth, bare skin. She'd left her hair down so that the curls tumbled over her shoulders, tempting him to slide his fingers into the soft tresses, tip her head back and cover that glossy mouth with his own.

He curled his fingers into his palms to resist the urge to reach for her. Over the past few weeks, he'd had a lot of practice keeping a tight rein on his growing desire. Sure, they'd shared kisses—necessary to convince others that they were a couple, and maybe a few that weren't necessary or part of any illusion—but he'd been careful to ensure those kisses never went too far.

But he'd done what Kevin had challenged him to do— he'd maintained a relationship with one woman for more than two months. And if this was truly his last date with Alyssa, he was going to make the most of it.

He pulled her into his arms.

"Um...hello," she said when he finally eased his lips from hers.

He smiled. "Hi." Then stepped back to look at her again. "And thank you."

She smiled back, a little tentatively. "I didn't own anything red, so I went shopping. Sky helped me pick this out."

"I guess even Gilmores get something right once in a while," he said.

She huffed out a breath. "For a few hours tonight, can you please try to forget about the feud between the Blakes and the Gilmores?"

"Why?"

"Because Liam's going to be at the wedding."

"I thought he might be," Jay admitted. "Though why anyone would want to watch an ex marry someone else is beyond me."

"Liam and Carrie dated a long time ago and have remained good friends."

"I don't get that, either," he said.

"You've never stayed friends with a girl you've dated?"

He thought about the question, shook his head. "Not friendly enough to want her at my wedding."

Alyssa looked taken aback by his comment.

"Is that really so surprising?" he asked.

"What surprised me was to hear the words *my wedding* come out of your mouth without your face draining of all color."

"Ha ha," he said.

"I wasn't joking," she told him.

Considering his reputation—and nickname—her response was understandable.

But Jason wasn't that man anymore.

And tonight he was going to focus his efforts on charming the only woman he wanted.

## Chapter Sixteen

The ceremony was short and sweet. The bride walked down the aisle with her father, then exchanged vows with her groom. After the minister pronounced them married, they kissed, signed the register and walked out of the church again.

At the reception, the meal was served family style, with the salad course followed by heaping bowls of pasta, then platters of thinly sliced roast beef and breaded chicken cutlets, plus bowls of roasted potatoes, green beans and baby carrots. Conversation flowed as freely as the wine, and Alyssa found herself enjoying the interactions between Jason and his friends.

After dessert—a choice of cheesecake or a slice of the wedding cake—the bride and groom shared their first dance, then the floor was opened up to the rest of the guests.

Alyssa had danced with Jason before, but being in his

arms felt different tonight. Or maybe she felt different—nervous and determined.

"What are you thinking about?" he asked, his lips close to her ear.

"I was just wondering if it was true, what Kevin said at dinner," she admitted.

"Kevin did a lot of talking at dinner," he remarked.

"I was referring to his claim that Jenny Reashore broke your heart."

He shook his head. "Not true."

"But she was the girl who dumped you before you asked Lacey Bolton to the homecoming dance?"

"Yeah," he admitted. "But we were seventeen—neither of us thought we were going to be together forever."

"So how long were you together?" she asked him.

He lifted a shoulder, as if he didn't remember.

"How long?" she pressed.

"Eight months."

"And how long were you with Melanie—that girl in college?"

"Five months."

"So your longest relationship was when you were seventeen?"

"How about you?" he challenged. "According to your grandmother, you haven't let anyone get close since your high school graduation party at the beach."

"She told you that?"

"The question is—why didn't *you* tell me?"

"I told you about what happened at the beach," she reminded him. "And that's more than I've ever told anyone else."

He was quiet for a minute, as if considering that admission. "You're an amazing woman, Lys, and I hate to think that you'd let anything that happened in the past hold you back from what you want now."

"I'm trying not to," she said.

"Good."

As the music changed, Alyssa found herself wondering if Jason's response would be the same if he knew that what she wanted now was him—and if she ever would find the courage to go after what she wanted.

They danced and they talked and they danced some more. When Alyssa slipped away to the ladies' room, Jay went to the bar to refill their drinks.

"I didn't think you'd pull it off," Nat admitted, joining him at the counter.

"You know I never back away from a challenge," he told her.

"So you've dated Alyssa for a few months and brought her as your date to Matt's wedding—now what?"

He accepted his drinks from the bartender. "Now I'm going to take this glass of wine to my date."

"There's no need to rush," she said. "She looks like she's enjoying herself on the dance floor."

He glanced over his shoulder and discovered that Nat was right. Alyssa had returned and was dancing again—with Gilmore. It wasn't a slow dance and it wasn't just the two of them, but Jay didn't appreciate the other man shaking and shimmying with *his* date. But Alyssa had requested that he forget about the feud for one night, so he deliberately loosened his grip on the glass before the stem broke in his hand.

"I understand the reasons for your proximity rule," Nat said to him now. "But sometimes there are good reasons to break the rules."

His gaze moved back to Alyssa again.

"You can thank me now," she said.

"I'm starting to think maybe I should," he acknowledged.

"Maybe? Why only maybe?"

"Because I'm not entirely sure where we go from here."

"You need me to draw you a map?"

He knew she was joking, and yet he didn't think it was such a bad idea. He was usually sure of all his moves when it came to the opposite sex, but it had been a very long time since anyone had mattered to him as much as Alyssa did. If anyone ever had.

"I think I can wing it," he said with more confidence than he felt.

"Just don't make the mistake of comparing her to any one of the legions of women who have come before," she cautioned.

"There haven't been legions of women," he denied.

She lifted a brow.

"And what is a legion, anyway?"

"A very large number," Kevin chimed in as he joined them. Then he nodded to Jay. "You and Alyssa look good together. Not just good, but happy."

"We're having fun," he confirmed.

"Maybe we'll be dancing at your wedding next."

"Bite your tongue," Jay said, though the knee-jerk response was made without heat.

"Fifty bucks says he's down on one knee before Christmas," Nat said.

"The way he looks at her, I'd wager it happens before Thanksgiving," Kevin said.

Jay shook his head. "Do you guys really have nothing better to do than bet on my love life?"

"Not at the moment," Nat said.

"Although we could go dance," Kevin said to her.

She did a double take. "What?"

"I'm asking if you want to dance with me."

"Where's your date?"

"Dancing with yours," he said. "So why should we be left out?"

Nat let Kevin lead her to the dance floor—and Alyssa began to move away from the crowd. As she drew nearer, she smiled, and Jay felt his lips curve in response as an unexpected warmth filled his chest.

Yeah, he was going to have to thank Nat for her machinations.

But right now, he had more important things to do—and dancing with Alyssa was at the top of his list.

After the happy couple had slipped away to begin their honeymoon, the rest of the wedding guests began to disperse. When Jason asked Alyssa if she was ready to go, she lied and said yes. But the truth was, she didn't want her time with Jason to be at an end.

"I guess this is where I say good-night," he said after he'd walked her to her door. But his gaze slid over her in a way that somehow melted her bones even as it steeled her resolve.

"Or you could come in," she suggested as an alternative.

He waited a beat before responding. "For a drink?"

She shrugged, trying to appear casual. But her heart was pounding so loud and fast she was sure he could hear the echo of its beat bouncing off the walls. "If that's what you want."

"What do *you* want?" he asked her.

"I don't want the night to be over," she admitted.

He glanced at his watch. "Except that, technically, it already is."

"You're right. And you probably have an early morning, so forget I said anything." She fumbled for her keys. "Good night, Jason."

He stepped in front of the door, blocking her escape. "Tell me what you want, Alyssa."

She nibbled on her lip. It was now or never. And if she didn't go for it, she'd always wonder *what if.* Maybe he'd say no, and that would be horrible and humiliating. But if he said yes… Well, she really wanted to experience yes.

So she inhaled a steadying breath and said, "I want you to break your rules—just for tonight."

"I don't know that I can do that," he told her.

"Oh." She dropped her gaze, feeling horrible and humiliated and—

He tipped her chin up. "If I break my rules, it won't be for just one night. If I make love with you tonight, I don't think I'll be able to walk away in the morning."

"Oh," she said again as blossoming hope pushed all the negative feelings aside.

"I've wanted you for a long time," he confided. "Even when I told myself that I shouldn't. But now that I know you want me, too, there's only one question remaining."

"What's that?" she asked breathlessly.

He smiled. "Your place or mine?"

Alyssa answered that question by turning the key to unlock her door. And when he followed her inside and drew her into his embrace, she went willingly, even eagerly. Her arms lifted to twine behind his head; her lips parted to welcome his kiss.

She wanted this, she really did, but now that it was finally going to happen, she couldn't help but feel a little nervous and uncertain.

Jason, sensing her hesitation, pulled back. "Second thoughts?" he asked gently.

"No," she said. Then, "Maybe."

"Can you explain that?"

"I don't want anything that happens tonight to change things between us."

"Things have already changed."

"You're right," she acknowledged. "I know you're right. I just wish you could promise me that things won't get weird."

"I don't usually bring out the toys and props the first time I'm with a woman," he told her. "Plus, all that stuff is upstairs."

"You're teasing. I hope."

He smiled. "Yeah, I'm teasing. But maybe we should go upstairs—because I don't have any protection in my wallet."

"I've got some. Um, condoms, I mean. I picked them up when I was shopping," she said, because she had no intention of telling him that Sky had bought them.

Alyssa might not know a lot about seduction, but she was pretty sure that mentioning the name of another woman—particularly a woman whose family was at odds with his—would cool the heat between them more effectively than dumping a glass of ice water in his lap.

"In that case," he said and kissed her again.

She started to move down the hall, toward her bedroom, not letting her lips break contact with his. Because as long as he was kissing her, she wasn't able to think about what was happening, which meant that she couldn't focus on all the doubts and insecurities that usually reared up when she got close to someone.

She felt as if they'd been moving toward this for weeks, maybe months. Even when she'd told herself they were just friends, she'd wanted more. Wanted this. Through months of fake dating and their seven-day engagement, the pretend stuff had stirred real desires. But she'd been certain it was all one-sided, until the morning she'd awakened in his arms and discovered he was aroused.

Of course, a lot of men, particularly those in their sexual prime, woke up with erections. But Jason had seemed to credit—or maybe blame—her proximity for his condition. As if he wasn't just aroused but aroused *by her*. And that was when the first seeds of this seduction plan began to take root in her mind.

His hands skimmed up her back now, making her shiver. He found the zipper at the back of her dress and inched it downward. The straps slid off her shoulders and she instinctively lifted a hand to hold the bodice in place.

He caught her wrist and drew it away. "No more hiding, Lys. Not from me."

The fabric fell away, revealing the scarlet lace bra that—along with the matching bikini panties—cost half as much as the dress.

He tugged the zipper the rest of the way, and the dress slipped over her hips to pool on the floor at her feet, leaving her clad in only red lace and three-inch heels.

He swore softly, reverently. "It's a good thing I didn't know what you were wearing under that dress when I picked you up, or we never would have made it to the wedding."

"I'm happy we got to see your friends get married," she said. "I'm even happier that you're here with me now."

His fingertip traced the lacy edge of her bra, skimming over the swell of one breast, dipping into the hollow between them, then back up again. He reached behind her with his other hand, deftly unclasping the hook and discarding the garment. Then he hooked his fingers into the sides of her panties and tugged them over her hips, then down her legs. When she was completely naked, he stripped away his own clothes, then eased her back onto the bed.

She closed her eyes to better absorb the myriad of sensations that assailed her as his hands and lips moved over her. She'd never been touched like he was touching her. Had never imagined that she was capable of feeling so much. And every time she thought there couldn't possibly be more, he proved otherwise.

She'd read books, she'd seen movies, but none of that had prepared her for the exquisite sensations that ricocheted through her body, sparking new wants, igniting new desires. His hands were strong and sure as they moved over her, knowing just where and how to touch her.

He cupped her breasts in his hands, his thumbs stroking lazily over her nipples. His touch triggered an unexpected response between her thighs, making her throb and ache. Then his mouth replaced his thumbs, and as he suckled at one breast, then the other, the ache intensified.

As his mouth continued its sensual assault on her breasts, his hands moved lower, skimming her sides, sliding over her hips, arrowing toward the juncture of her thighs. He continued his leisurely exploration, sucking in a breath as his thumbs slowly traced the narrow strip of hair that was all that remained after her French bikini wax.

His thumbs parted the slick folds of skin, exposing her most sensitive core to his gaze. His touch. His mouth.

Her head fell back as his tongue stroked over her.

Slowly. Gently.

Then faster. Harder.

She tried to draw in a breath, but there was no air—there was nothing but sharp, shocking pleasure.

She curled her fingers in the sheet, bit down on her lip. His hands slid under her bottom, holding her in position while he did unexpectedly wicked and wonderful things to her with his mouth, while every dip and flick of his tongue drove her closer and closer to the edge of oblivion.

For the first time in years, she had cause to worry about the condition of her heart. She'd never felt it beat so hard and fast. She didn't know that it could without leaping right out of her chest or at least cracking a few ribs.

But she didn't ask him to stop. She didn't want him to stop. And then the wonderful, glorious sensations built to a crescendo of light and color that exploded inside her like Fourth of July fireworks. A seemingly endless grand finale that left her breathless and weak.

She closed her eyes as delicious shudders rippled through her and he slowly made his way up her body, dropping leisurely kisses along the way. On her belly, her navel, the hollow beneath her breastbone, the pale scar between her breasts. And her heart, having slowed to a more natural rhythm, stuttered.

"Okay?" he asked.

Her lips curved. "Much better than okay."

"Good."

He kissed her throat, then the underside of her jaw, then her lips.

"Is it my turn now?" she asked.

His laugh was strangled. "No. Not tonight."

"Why not?"

"Because it's been a long time since I've been with a woman and I'm already doubting my ability to last more than three minutes."

"But you've already given me so much more than I expected," she told him.

"Then your expectations were way too low, because we're not even close to being done yet."

As he was talking, he tore open a square packet and covered himself with a condom. He nudged her legs apart and positioned himself between them, and everything inside her trembled with anticipation. She wasn't just eager now but desperate for the fulfillment she instinctively knew he could give her. She wanted to feel the hard length of him inside her, stretching her, filling her.

He rose over her, bracing his weight on his forearms as his lips brushed hers gently and his erection nudged her soft flesh, testing, teasing. The ache inside her turned to need, and she drew her knees up and dug her heels into the mattress. "Now," she said. "Please."

He didn't make her ask again. In one deep stroke, he pushed into her. She gasped at the shock of the intrusion as he broke through the barrier of her virginity. He stopped moving. In fact, he went totally and completely still.

She knew that she should say something, but there were no words to express what she was feeling. No words to describe the unexpected thrill of feeling him buried deep inside her, of the glorious sensations that battered her from all directions.

Instead, she let her instincts take over, lifting her hips off the mattress, pulling him deeper, urging him on. He swore through gritted teeth as he gave up the fight for control and let her desire—and his own—carry them both toward the pinnacle of pleasure.

## *Chapter Seventeen*

He rolled off her and onto his back, fighting to catch his breath and struggling to figure out what the hell had just happened. But it was difficult to think when his brain cells seemed incapable of the most basic functions.

"What the—"

Alyssa winced at the expletive he used to complete the sentence.

Jay didn't care. He said it again. And again.

"Don't you think you're overreacting a little?" she interjected as she shifted away from him, dragging the top sheet with her.

"No, I don't think I'm overreacting." He practically shouted the words at her. "My God, Lys—you were a virgin."

She didn't cower from his anger. In fact, she squared her shoulders and faced him defiantly, wearing nothing more than the bedsheet she held clenched in a fist between her breasts. "So?"

He found his briefs in the pile of discarded clothing on the floor and yanked them on. "So you should have told me."

*And he should have known.*

The clues were all there, if he'd bothered to take the time to piece them together. But when she'd invited him into her bedroom, he'd been focused on the finish line to the exclusion of all else. He'd not only taken her virginity, he'd done so with little thought and even less care, and the realization burned in his gut.

"Why?" she demanded in response to his claim.

He couldn't believe she would have to ask such a question. "Because that's not the kind of information a guy wants to discover *after* he's irrevocably changed the status."

"You're making this into a bigger deal than it is," she said, clearly unconvinced by his argument.

"It *is* a big deal."

She shook her head. "You don't understand."

"Explain it to me," he suggested.

She took a minute to wrap the sheet around herself before perching on the edge of the mattress. "All my life, I've been handled with kid gloves. There were so many things I wasn't allowed to do, so many experiences I missed out on, because my heart was fragile."

He scowled at that. "You told me your heart was fine."

"My heart *is* fine," she said. "But no matter how many doctors said exactly that, my parents refused to believe it. As a result, I led a very sheltered life.

"Yeah, I dated some, but whenever I started to get close to somebody—close enough to tell them about my surgeries, to prepare them for seeing my scars—their romantic interest inevitably gave way to a morbid fascination, and it was suddenly all about a birth defect that had stopped being relevant to me a long time ago. No one ever treated me like I was normal—until you."

He could hardly dispute what she was saying. He had no experience comparable to hers.

"Maybe it wouldn't have made a difference," she continued. "But maybe it would have, and I didn't want to take that chance. I was tired of feeling like a freak because I was a twenty-six-year-old virgin."

His fury was justified—she'd deliberately withheld important information. But it was difficult to hold on to his righteous anger in the face of the hurt and frustration he heard in her voice. "You're not a freak, Alyssa," he told her. "You're an incredibly smart, sweet, sexy woman."

"I was a twenty-six-year-old virgin," she said again.

"You're not that anymore," he pointed out.

That earned him a small smile. "I'm sorry I didn't tell you."

"Are you?" he wondered aloud.

"Well, I'm sorry that you were mad I didn't tell you," she clarified.

"I guess, under the circumstances, I can kind of understand," he agreed.

"But I wasn't only afraid that you'd treat me differently," she admitted now. "I was afraid…"

He sat on the edge of the bed, beside her. "Tell me."

She took a minute, as if to find the words she needed to express her feelings, then let them out in a rush. "I was afraid if you knew about my lack of experience you wouldn't want me."

He lifted a hand to her face, gently tipped her chin up so that she had to meet his gaze. "Apparently you're not as smart as I thought you were."

Hers showed confusion.

"How could you possibly think I wouldn't want you?" he asked, his tone softer now.

"I know you've had a lot of girlfriends," she said. "Girlfriends who undoubtedly had a lot more—"

He touched a finger to her lips, silencing her. "Let's keep this between you and me," he suggested.

"I don't want you to feel responsible for me…because of what just happened. I knew what I was doing when I asked you to stay," she said. "I didn't do it to try to turn a pretend relationship into something real."

"I'm feeling a lot of things," he acknowledged, "but responsible isn't one of them."

"What are you feeling?"

"Right now, looking at your sexy body wrapped in nothing more than that sheet, I'd say that 'aroused' is at the top of the list."

Her eyes widened. "Does that mean… Can we do it again?"

He chuckled softly. "Oh, yeah," he said. "I think it's safe to say we can do it again—"

A smile curved her lips.

"—but maybe not tonight."

The smile faded. "Why not? I've got a whole box of condoms."

And damn if that reminder didn't make him want to use every last one before the morning sun peeked over the horizon. But despite her evident enthusiasm, and his own eagerness, he had to remember that her body had been untouched and might be feeling more tender than she realized.

"Because I don't want to hurt you any more," he told her.

"You didn't hurt me," she said. "There was a brief twinge—and then there was nothing but pleasure. I want you to make me feel that way again."

"And to think that I once questioned your ability to negotiate," he mused ruefully.

Her lips curved again. "Does that mean you'll come back to bed with me?"

He didn't know how to deny her what they both wanted, so he didn't even try.

Alyssa hadn't expected any more than one night.

Especially when she saw how angry Jason was after the first time they'd made love, she didn't think anything she said or did would allow him to forgive her. But she was starting to realize that being a woman was a powerful thing—and she was enjoying wielding that power.

She knew that a woman's first time wasn't always pleasant. More often it was awkward and painful—and it didn't always get better after that.

It had admittedly taken her body a little while to adjust to the intrusion of his, but that little bit of discomfort had been eclipsed by the pleasure he gave her, both before and after. That first experience had been wonderful. Certainly she hadn't expected that it could get any better than that.

She'd been wrong.

Shockingly and fabulously wrong, as he proved to her night after night.

In the mornings, they resumed running together—although they sometimes got a later start, opting to begin the day with a different kind of cardio workout before they laced up their running shoes and hit the pavement.

Now Jason wasn't just her running partner, he was her friend and her lover.

*She had a lover.*

The knowledge made her giddy.

The memories of what he could and had done to her in the bedroom made her even giddier.

She didn't let herself worry about the future or even try to define their relationship because she'd never been happier than she was with Jason.

Every morning that Alyssa woke beside him, she was grateful for everything she had. She'd hoped for one night. A few hours to finally rid herself of the virgin label that chafed like an ill-fitting bra. A few hours to feel desire and desired, to experience passion.

That one night turned into two and then three. Then days became weeks. She was on summer break from school but continued to work at Diggers' and picked up additional shifts when they were offered. If she had to close the bar, Jason would meet her there, unwilling to spend even one night apart from her. Alyssa didn't complain.

She did wonder about the changes that would come along with the end of summer—when he had more free time and she had less. So far, their relationship had been mostly fun and games—which was, she knew, the only kind of relationship he had.

But with every day that passed, every minute they were together, her feelings for him continued to grow. She loved being with him. She loved his company and companionship. She loved the intimacies they shared—the way he made her feel when he touched her and kissed her, when their bodies moved together.

But even though she knew she was teetering on the edge, her heart precariously balanced, she held herself back from falling in love with him. She was smarter than that, stronger than that. And when he decided it was over, she would be grateful for the experience he'd shared with her.

She wouldn't be picking up pieces of a broken heart.

Three weeks after Matt's wedding—after the first night he'd spent with Alyssa—Jay finally acknowledged that his life had drastically veered off the course he'd set. But it hadn't happened that night. No, it was a process that had started months earlier—the first night that Alyssa kissed him.

It was crazy how much he wanted her. Never stopped wanting her. His friends weren't wrong in claiming there was a pattern to his relationships, and this romance should have run its course long before now.

But Alyssa was unlike any other woman he'd ever known. She was interesting and fun, beautiful and passionate, and he couldn't bring himself to contemplate the end of their relationship. He didn't want to imagine a future without her in it.

That was when he finally recognized the truth that had been staring him in the eye for weeks. Alyssa was more than a temporary girlfriend, fake fiancée or current lover—she was the woman he loved.

Now he just had to convince her to give their pretend relationship a real chance for a happy ending.

On a Sunday afternoon, two weeks before the end of summer, Alyssa was weeding the flower garden in the backyard when a shadow suddenly blocked out the sun.

"Diego, this is a surprise." She hadn't heard a single word from him since she'd left California, so his appearance here now was definitely unexpected.

He smiled. "I was in Reno for a friend's wedding and decided, since I was in the neighborhood, I'd stop by to see you."

"Reno is two hundred and fifty miles away," she noted. "That's hardly in the neighborhood."

"It's a lot closer than Irvine," he pointed out.

"True," she acknowledged, wiping the dirt from her hands on the thighs of her jeans. Her hair was on top of her head in a haphazard ponytail, strands falling out around a face bare of makeup, and the scoop-neck T-shirt she wore dipped low between her breasts.

A few months earlier, she might have worried about her appearance. She certainly would have tugged at the neckline of her shirt to cover her scars. But being with Jason had helped her be a lot more comfortable in her own skin and a lot less concerned about the judgments of others.

Still, she couldn't deny that this situation made her feel awkward and uncomfortable. She hadn't invited Diego and she certainly didn't want him here, but she could hardly turn him away without at least offering him a beverage after he'd come so far to see her. Unannounced and uninvited, but still…

"Can I get you a cold drink?" she asked.

"I'll have a soda, if it's not too much trouble," he decided.

"Have a seat." She gestured to the arrangement of wicker furniture. "I'll be right back."

She hurried inside and grabbed a cola for Diego and a bottle of water for herself. Then she took a few extra minutes to slice some cheese and set it on a plate with some crackers. Not that she wanted to encourage him to stay, but his family was close to hers and her mother would be appalled if Alyssa didn't offer some basic hospitality. Then she added some grapes to the plate, because her grandmother's lessons about presentation were as deeply ingrained as her mother's about manners.

"It's a long drive from Reno, and I thought you might be hungry," she said, setting the plate down along with his cola.

"I didn't realize I was until you put that out," he said.

She sipped her water while he snacked and shared some of the highlights from the wedding he'd attended.

"What are your plans now?" she asked when he'd put his plate aside. "Are you staying with your cousin in Elko?"

"No. I stopped at the Dusty Boots Motel and booked a room on my way into town."

"I spent a few nights there when I first came to Haven. It's not fancy, but it's clean and, until Liam Gilmore gets the old Stagecoach Inn open, it's the only local option. Plus, the diner does a decent breakfast, so you can fuel up before you start back in the morning."

"I was actually thinking I might stay in Nevada for a few more days," he told her. "I didn't get to see much of Haven—or you—on my last visit, and I'm hoping this time will be different."

"Oh…um, I guess I could give you a quick tour of the town," she offered.

"Or a not-so-quick tour," he suggested hopefully.

Alyssa capped her water bottle and set it on the table as she considered what to say to him—and decided that, since subtlety hadn't worked, she'd have to be blunt.

"Diego, if I ever said or did anything to mislead you, I sincerely apologize," she said. "And if my mother gave you any hope of a romantic relationship between us, I'm sorry about that, too. You're a terrific guy, really, but I don't have any romantic feelings for you."

He frowned at his cola. "This is because of that Jason guy, isn't it?"

"Even if I wasn't with Jason, I wouldn't be with you," she told him, trying for a gentle tone to dull the sharp edge of her words.

"I've been in love with you since I was fifteen," Diego admitted.

"I believe you might have had a crush on me—"

"It's more than that," he insisted. "I dated other girls, of course, but my heart has always belonged to you—even if you didn't know it. And when Renata invited me to the New Year's Eve party, I knew that she wanted us to be together as much as I did."

Alyssa couldn't deny that was probably true, at least at the time, so she focused on the present. "But it wasn't what *I* wanted. It's *not* what *I* want."

"You want Jason," he said bitterly.

She wanted to make her own choices and live her own life, but if Diego needed a scapegoat, she wasn't going to belabor the point. She just wanted him to go away so that she didn't have to feel guilty about putting that wounded look on his face.

"When you were in California for your parents' anniversary party, he told me that he'd asked you to marry him," Diego continued. "And that you'd said yes."

She nodded, not claiming the proposal had actually happened, but confirming his summary of the conversation.

"I commented then—and can't help noticing now—that you're not wearing a ring on your finger."

"Which isn't a big deal to anyone but you."

"If he's dragging his heels, that should be a warning that he's not committed to the idea of marriage—or to you."

"He hasn't been dragging his heels," she said. "We're just not in a hurry to start making plans."

"What aren't we making plans for?" Jason asked.

Alyssa started at the sound of his voice.

She'd been so focused on trying to make Diego see the futility of his romantic dreams that she hadn't heard Jason's truck pull into the driveway.

"Your wedding," Diego said in response to the question.

Jason moved over to where she was seated and bent to brush a light but lingering kiss on her lips. She knew it wasn't a gesture of affection so much as a brand of possession, and the Neanderthal display should have put her back up. But as always happened whenever Jason kissed her, she melted just a little.

"I was thinking a Christmas wedding," Jason said in a conversational tone. "But Alyssa wants to wear Valentina's wedding dress, and the alterations might take some time."

She was surprised that he knew about her desire to wear her grandmother's gown, but that knowledge finally seemed to convince Diego that Jason was committed to his supposed bride-to-be despite the absence of a ring on her finger.

"You will be the most beautiful bride," Diego said to Alyssa as he rose to his feet. "And I sincerely hope you only cry tears of joy on your wedding day."

"He has a point," Jason noted when the other man had gone.

"About what?" she wondered, shocked that he'd agree with Diego about anything.

"No one is ever going to believe that we're planning to get married unless I put a ring on your finger."

"Because we're not actually planning to get married," she pointed out.

"But maybe we should," he said.

She stared at him, wary and a little concerned. "Did you fall off the rock wall and hit your head today?"

"I'm not concussed or brain damaged," he assured her.

"Well, that's the only explanation I can think of for those words to have come out of your mouth."

"How about this one—I've fallen in love with you," he suggested.

## *Chapter Eighteen*

Maybe she was the one who'd hit her head, because she was certain he hadn't just spoken the words she'd heard. "Are we having a hypothetical conversation?"

"No, Alyssa. I'm trying to tell you that I have real feelings for you, and I think—*I hope*—you have real feelings for me, too."

She did. Of course she did. But his declaration was as unexpected to her as Diego's visit.

"I want to end the pretense and be with you for real," he continued. "I want to marry you for real."

"Ohmygod." It was a good thing she was already sitting down, because the bones in her legs felt as if they'd completely melted away.

"I was expecting a yes or no answer," he told her. "Preferably a yes."

"This wasn't supposed to be real," she felt compelled to remind him.

"And yet this entire charade was more real than any other relationship I've ever had. My feelings for you are more real than anything I've ever felt for anyone else."

She'd never expected to hear him say those words. Words that filled her heart with so much unspeakable joy she felt as if it actually swelled inside her chest.

Except that this wasn't what she wanted. She'd moved to Nevada to be independent, and she was finally starting to get the hang of it. She wasn't ready to fall in love and build a life with someone else—not even the man she suspected she loved already.

"You said that our fake relationship wasn't going to turn into anything more," she reminded him. "You *promised.*"

The desperation in her tone was Jay's first clue that this wasn't going to go as he'd imagined. "I didn't plan to fall in love with you," he said patiently. "It just happened."

"Then maybe you can fall out of love with me just as spontaneously," she suggested.

"I don't think so," he said, ruefully acknowledging that any illusions he had of her throwing herself into his arms and professing undying love were nothing more than that.

"You could at least try."

"I don't want to try. I want to be with you."

"What happened to not wanting to emulate your parents' marriage?" she asked.

"I'm not worried about that anymore. Not with you." He took her hands, linked their fingers together. "What are you afraid of, Lys?" he asked gently.

"Marriage is a promise. A commitment." She shook her head. "I can't."

He released her hands and leaned back against the rock wall bordering the patio. "You're serious," he realized. "You're actually saying no."

"I have to. I'm not ready for this," she said. "Not right now."

His wounded pride urged him to walk away. No way in hell was he going to beg for scraps of affection. But his pride was no match for his heart, demanding that he hold on to hope. "When?"

She looked at him, her eyes filled with anguish and tears. "I don't know. And I'm not asking you to wait for me—that wouldn't be fair."

"You're right," he agreed. "But I'm not going anywhere, Alyssa. Because I love you, and I know now that real love doesn't just go away. So when you decide that you're ready to share your heart—and your life—I'll be right here waiting for you."

Alyssa went back to California for a week before school was scheduled to resume. She needed time away from Jason, and not just distance but perspective, to help her get her head on straight—and she desperately needed to get her head on straight. Because it didn't matter where she was or who she was with; she was always thinking about him. And, of course, the whole time she was in Irvine, she remembered her last visit—with Jason.

She didn't like to think that it might be her heart rather than her head that was the problem. But she couldn't deny that she missed him unbearably.

Still, she was sure she'd done the right thing. Whatever she was feeling now was only temporary. They'd both been caught up in the play—like actors who fell in love while working together on the stage, only to find those feelings fade when they went their separate ways.

When were the feelings going to fade?

When was she going to wake up and not miss him?

Three days later, when she still didn't have the answers to those questions, she went to see her sister and confided, "Jason asked me to marry him."

Cristina, who'd been as hurt as she was disappointed to learn her sister's engagement was a sham, paused with her cup of coffee halfway to her mouth. "For real this time?"

Alyssa nodded. "But I said no."

Her sister's brows lifted. "Why?"

"Because it seemed a slightly less terrifying option than saying yes," she admitted.

Cristina sipped her coffee, considering. "Do you love him?"

"How would I know?" she asked. "I've never been in love before."

"So you don't think anyone who falls in love only once can ever be sure that it's real?"

"Of course not," she replied. "But even if this is real, I'm not ready for it. I've only just started to live my own life."

"And you think being in a committed relationship with a man who loves and respects you will somehow jeopardize your independence?"

"I don't know," she admitted.

"Okay, let me ask you this—do you think I'm less myself since I married Steven?"

"Of course not. But you've always been brave, strong and independent, able to tackle any obstacles in your path."

"And you think you've been scared, weak and dependent?" her sister guessed.

"I have been," she insisted. "Isn't that why you encouraged me to move away from Irvine?"

Cristina shook her head. "I encouraged you to move away so that you could see the truth—that you're every bit as brave and strong and independent as I am. Maybe even more so, because you've overcome obstacles I've never had to face."

Alyssa swiped at a tear that spilled onto her cheek. "I'm not brave—I'm terrified."

"Of course you are. Because love is terrifying. And wonderful. And I'm so happy for you."

"I told him no," she reminded her sister.

"And when you go back to Haven, you'll tell him yes," Cristina said.

Alyssa didn't believe for a minute it could be that simple, but for the first time since she got on the plane in Elko, she felt a tiny blossom of hope unfurl inside her heart.

She'd been gone for five days.

And in those five days, Jason had received no communication from Alyssa. Not a phone call, not even a text message.

Of course, he hadn't contacted her, either.

But he'd picked up the phone so many times he'd lost count. And he'd started numerous text messages, only to delete each and every one before sending.

He'd already put his heart on the line—there wasn't anything more that he could do. He didn't want to pressure her. And he definitely didn't want to come across as a pathetically needy guy who couldn't accept that the woman he loved didn't love him back.

Because he didn't feel pathetic or needy—he just felt empty, as if there was a great big gaping hole in his life where she used to be.

Okay, maybe that was pathetic and needy. And when the knock sounded at his door, he jumped up to answer it, grateful for any interruption of his unwelcome thoughts and uncomfortable reflections.

Then he opened the door, and she was there. And his pathetically needy heart immediately filled with hope and joy, though his wounded pride and wary mind urged caution.

"You're back," he said and immediately felt like a fool for stating the obvious.

She nodded. "Have I come at a bad time?"

He had no idea what time it was, and he didn't care. All that mattered was that she was here. After five endless days, she was finally here.

But of course, he didn't say that to her. Instead, he responded with a shake of his head. "No, it's not a bad time."

She smiled, though it wavered a little. "Good, because I've been waiting for five days to tell you something and I don't want to wait even five minutes more."

"Do you want to come in or say it in the hall?"

She walked through the open door and into the sitting area, but she remained standing, so he did the same.

"For a long time, I honestly thought my damaged heart was incapable of falling in love," she confided. "Then I met you...and suddenly I was feeling all kinds of things I'd never felt before. And the more time we spent together, the more those feelings grew. I knew I was starting to fall for you—and it was the most exhilarating and terrifying feeling in the world. But I didn't want to go splat, so I held myself back.

"And maybe I was doing just fine, living my own life, but you showed me what it could be like to share my life with someone. With you. And I wanted that so much that it scared me. Because I didn't let myself hope that you might ever feel about me the way I felt about you, and I was certain the only thing that would be worse than never experiencing love would be trying to put together the broken pieces of my heart.

"You once told me that I was brave, but I'm not. I'm a coward. I was willing to walk away from the possibility of what we could have together rather than risk having my heart broken."

"You're here now," he pointed out.

"I'm here now," she agreed.

"And now that you've taken the first step, the next one should be a little easier," he said encouragingly.

But Alyssa was still wary. "The next one's not a step. It's a leap."

He held her gaze, and she could see the feelings in his heart reflected in his eyes. "I'll catch you," he promised.

And because she knew that he would, she leaped.

"I love you, Jason Channing. I didn't plan for this to happen—I didn't even want it to happen. But I trust now that my feelings are real and not going to change, and I don't want to spend even one more day without you. So, if you still love me—"

"I still love you," he assured her.

And the unwavering conviction in his tone made her smile come a little more easily this time.

But he wasn't finished yet. "These past few days without you have been the loneliest, emptiest days of my life," he continued. "I was perfectly content before you came along. I didn't want or need anything else, until you showed me how much better everything is when we're together.

"There was a time when the prospect of spending the rest of my days with one person made me panic. Now the only thing that scares me is the prospect of spending even a single day without you beside me. You are my everything—for now and forever."

She hadn't expected such an outpouring of emotion, but his words filled her heart to overflowing. "In that case, I would like to say yes to your proposal," she told him. "Because there's nothing I want more than to marry you and build a life with you—for now and forever."

He turned away from her then and made his way across the room to his desk. "I still don't have an engagement ring," he said as he opened the top drawer. "And Carter will no doubt curse a blue streak when I leave him in charge of Adventure Village again, but I want to take you to New York to pick one out."

At his mention of a ring, the last of the weight that had been sitting on her chest was lifted, allowing her to tease, "They don't sell engagement rings anywhere in Nevada?"

"They don't have Tiffany's flagship store in Nevada," he told her. "Plus, I know you've always wanted to see New York City and I'd really like you to meet Brie."

"I'd like that, too, but I don't need a piece of jewelry to…" Her words trailed off when he handed her the flat velvet box he'd retrieved from his desk.

"It's not a ring," he said again. "But maybe you can wear it as a symbol of my love for you until we get a diamond."

She took the box from him and carefully opened the lid to reveal a perfectly shaped heart pendant on a delicate gold chain. "Oh, Jason. It's beautiful."

"I'm not asking you to get rid of the necklace your sister gave you, but I'm hoping you'll wear this one sometimes and know that this is how I see your heart—whole and perfect."

"My heart's not perfect," she told him. "But I promise that it's yours. For now and forever."

And when he took her in his arms, she knew that her imperfect heart had finally found its perfect match.

\* \* \* \* \*

*Don't miss*
*SIX WEEKS TO CATCH A COWBOY*
*the next installment in Brenda Harlen's*
*new miniseries*

**MATCH MADE IN HAVEN**

*On sale September 2018*
*Available wherever*
*Harlequin books and ebooks are sold.*

*And catch up with the happenings in Haven, Nevada!*

*Look for*
*THE SHERIFF'S NINE-MONTH SURPRISE*
*On sale now.*

*Keep reading for a special preview of*
*HERONS LANDING,*
*the first in an exciting new series from*
New York Times *bestselling author*
*JoAnn Ross and HQN Books!*

# CHAPTER ONE

SETH HARPER WAS spending a Sunday spring afternoon detailing his wife's Rallye Red Honda Civic when he learned that she'd been killed by a suicide bomber in Afghanistan.

Despite the Pacific Northwest's reputation for unrelenting rain, the sun was shining so brightly that the Army notification officers—a man and a woman in dark blue uniforms and black shoes spit-shined to a mirror gloss—had been wearing shades. Or maybe, Seth considered, as they'd approached the driveway in what appeared to be slow motion, they would've worn them anyway. Like armor, providing emotional distance from the poor bastard whose life they were about to blow to smithereens.

At the one survivor grief meeting he'd later attended (only to get his fretting mother off his back), he'd heard stories from other spouses who'd experienced a sudden, painful jolt of loss before their official notice. Seth hadn't received any advance warning. Which was why, at first, the officers' words had been an incomprehensible buzz in his ears. Like distant radio static.

Zoe couldn't be dead. His wife wasn't a combat soldier. She was an Army surgical nurse, working in a heavily protected military base hospital, who'd be returning to civilian life in two weeks. Seth still had a bunch of stuff on his homecoming punch list to do. After buffing the wax off the Civic's hood and shining up the chrome wheels, his next project was to paint the walls white in the nursery he'd added on to their Folk Victorian cottage for the baby they'd be making.

She'd begun talking a lot about baby stuff early in her deployment. Although Seth was as clueless as the average guy about a woman's mind, it didn't take Dr. Phil to realize that she was using the plan to start a family as a touchstone. Something to hang on to during their separation.

In hours of Skype calls between Honeymoon Harbor and Kabul, they'd discussed the pros and cons of the various names on a list that had grown longer each time they'd talked. While the names remained up in the air, she *had* decided that whatever their baby's gender, the nursery should be a bright white to counter the Olympic Peninsula's gray skies.

She'd also sent him links that he'd dutifully followed to Pinterest pages showing bright crib bedding, mobiles and wooden name letters in primary crayon shades of blue, green, yellow and red. Even as Seth had lobbied for Seattle Seahawk navy and action green, he'd known that he'd end up giving his wife whatever she wanted.

The same as he'd been doing since the day he fell head over heels in love with her back in middle school.

Meanwhile, planning to get started on that baby making as soon as she got back to Honeymoon Harbor, he'd built the nursery as a welcome-home surprise.

Then Zoe had arrived at Sea-Tac airport in a flag-draped casket.

And two years after the worst day of his life, the room remained unpainted behind a closed door Seth had never opened since.

MANNION'S PUB & BREWERY was located on the street floor
of a faded redbrick building next to Honeymoon Harbor's
ferry landing. The former salmon cannery had been one
of many buildings constructed after the devastating 1893
fire that had swept along the waterfront, burning down the
original wood buildings. One of Seth's ancestors, Jacob
Harper, had built the replacement in 1894 for the town's
mayor and pub owner, Finn Mannion. Despite the inability
of Washington authorities to keep Canadian alcohol from
flooding into the state, the pub had been shuttered during
Prohibition in the 1930s, effectively putting the Mannions
out of the pub business until Quinn Mannion had returned
home from Seattle and hired Harper Construction to re-
claim the abandoned space.

Although the old Victorian seaport town wouldn't swing
into full tourist mode until Memorial Day, nearly every
table was filled when Seth dropped in at the end of the
day. He'd no sooner slid onto a stool at the end of the long
wooden bar when Quinn, who'd been washing glasses in
a sink, stuck a bottle of Shipwreck CDA in front of him.

"Double cheddar bacon or stuffed blue cheese?" he
asked.

"Double cheddar bacon." As he answered the question,
it crossed Seth's mind that his life—what little he had outside his work of restoring the town's Victorian buildings
constructed by an earlier generation of Harpers—had possibly slid downhill beyond routine to boringly predictable.
"And don't bother boxing it up. I'll be eating it here," he
added.

Quinn lifted a dark brow. "I didn't see that coming."

Meaning that, by having dinner here at the pub six
nights a week, the seventh being with Zoe's parents—
where they'd recount old memories, and look through
scrapbooks of photos that continued to cause an ache deep

in his heart—he'd undoubtedly landed in the predictable zone. So, what was wrong with that? Predictability was an underrated concept. By definition, it meant a lack of out-of-the-blue surprises that might destroy life as you knew it. Some people might like change. Seth was not one of them. Which was why he always ordered takeout with his first beer of the night.

The second beer he drank at home with his burger and fries. While other guys in his position might have escaped reality by hitting the bottle, Seth always stuck to a limit of two bottles, beginning with that long, lonely dark night after burying his wife. Because, although he'd never had a problem with alcohol, he harbored a secret fear that if he gave in to the temptation to begin seriously drinking, he might never stop.

The same way if he ever gave in to the anger, the unfairness of what the hell had happened, he'd have to patch a lot more walls in his house than he had those first few months after the notification officers' arrival.

There'd been times when he'd decided that someone in the Army had made a mistake. That Zoe hadn't died at all. Maybe she'd been captured during a melee and no one knew enough to go out searching for her. Or perhaps she was lying in some other hospital bed, her face all bandaged, maybe with amnesia, or even in a coma, and some lab tech had mixed up blood samples with another soldier who'd died. That could happen, right?

But as days slid into weeks, then weeks into months, he'd come to accept that his wife really was gone. Most of the time. Except when he'd see her, from behind, strolling down the street, window-shopping or walking onto the ferry, her dark curls blowing into a frothy tangle. He'd embarrassed himself a couple times by calling out her name. Now he never saw her at all. And worse yet, less and less in his memory. Zoe was fading away. Like that ghost who reputedly haunted Herons Landing, the old Victorian mansion up on the bluff overlooking the harbor.

"I'm having dinner with Mom tonight." And had been dreading it all the damn day. Fortunately, his dad hadn't heard about it yet. But since news traveled at the speed of sound in Honeymoon Harbor, he undoubtedly soon would.

"You sure you don't want to wait to order until she gets here?"

"She's not eating here. It's a command-performance dinner," he said. "To have dinner with her and the guy who may be her new boyfriend. Instead of eating at her new apartment, she decided that it'd be better to meet on neutral ground."

"Meaning somewhere other than a brewpub owned and operated by a Mannion," Quinn said. "Especially given the rumors that said new boyfriend just happens to be my uncle Mike."

"That does make the situation stickier." Seth took a long pull on the Cascadian Dark Ale and wished it was something stronger.

The feud between the Harpers and Mannions dated back to the early 1900s. After having experienced a boom during the end of the nineteenth century, the once-bustling seaport town had fallen on hard times during a national financial depression.

Although the population declined drastically, those dreamers who'd remained were handed a stroke of luck in 1910 when the newlywed king and queen of Montacroix added the town to their honeymoon tour of America. The couple had learned of this lush green region from the king's friend Theodore Roosevelt, who'd set aside national land for the Mount Olympus Monument.

As a way of honoring the royals, and hoping that the national and European press following them across the country might bring more attention to the town, residents had voted nearly unanimously to change the name to Honeymoon Harbor. Seth's ancestor Nathaniel Harper had been the lone holdout, creating acrimony on both sides that continued to linger among some but not all of the citizens. Quinn's father, after all, was a Mannion, his mother a Harper. But Ben Harper, Seth's father, tended to nurse his grudges. Even century-old ones that had nothing to do with him. Or at least hadn't. Until lately.

"And it gets worse," he said.

"Okay."

One of the things that made Quinn such a good bartender was that he listened a lot more than he talked. Which made Seth wonder how he'd managed to spend all those years as a big-bucks corporate lawyer in Seattle before returning home to open this pub and microbrewery.

"The neutral location she chose is Leaf."

Quinn's quick laugh caused two women who were drinking wine at a table looking out over the water to glance up with interest. Which wasn't surprising. Quinn's brother Wall Street wizard Gabe Mannion might be richer, New York City pro quarterback Burke Mannion flashier, and, last time he'd seen him, which had admittedly been a while, Marine-turned-LA-cop Aiden Mannion had still carried that bad-boy vibe that had gotten him in trouble a lot while they'd been growing up together. But Quinn's superpower had always been the ability to draw the attention of females—from bald babies in strollers to blue-haired elderly women in walkers—without seeming to do a thing.

After turning in the burger order, and helping out his waitress by delivering meals to two of the tables, Quinn returned to the bar and began hanging up the glasses.

"Let me guess," he said. "You ordered the burger as an

appetizer before you go off to a vegetarian restaurant to dine on alfalfa sprouts and pretty flowers."

"It's a matter of survival. I spent the entire day until I walked in here taking down a wall, adding a new reinforcing beam and framing out a bathroom. A guy needs sustenance. Not a plate of arugula and pansies."

"Since I run a place that specializes in pub grub, you're not going to get any argument from me on that plan. Do you still want the burger to go for the mutt?"

Bandit, a black Lab/boxer mix so named for his penchant for stealing food from Seth's construction sites back in his stray days—including once gnawing through a canvas ice chest—usually waited patiently in the truck for his burger. Tonight Seth had dropped him off at the house on his way over here, meaning the dog would have to wait a little longer for his dinner. Not that he hadn't mooched enough from the framers already today. If the vet hadn't explained strays' tendencies for overeating because they didn't know where their next meal might be coming from, Seth might have suspected the street-scarred dog he'd rescued of having a tapeworm.

They shot the breeze while Quinn served up drinks, which in this place ran more to the craft beer he brewed in the building next door. A few minutes later, the swinging door to the kitchen opened and out came two layers of prime beef topped with melted local cheddar cheese, bacon and caramelized grilled onions, with a slice of tomato and an iceberg-lettuce leaf tossed in as an apparent nod to the food pyramid, all piled between the halves of an oversize toasted kaiser bun. Taking up the rest of the heated metal platter was a mountain of spicy French fries.

Next to the platter was a take-out box of plain burger. It wouldn't stay warm, but having first seen the dog scroung-

ing from a garbage can on the waterfront, Seth figured
Bandit didn't care about the temperature of his dinner.

"So, you're eating in tonight," a bearded giant wearing
a T-shirt with Embrace the Lard on the front said in a deep
foghorn voice. "I didn't see that coming."

"Everyone's a damn joker," Seth muttered, even as
the aroma of grilled beef and melted cheese drew him
in. He took a bite and nearly moaned. The Norwegian,
who'd given up cooking on fishing boats when he'd gotten tired of freezing his ass off during winter crabbing
season, might be a sarcastic smart-ass, but the guy sure
as hell could cook.

"He's got a dinner date tonight at Leaf." Quinn, for
some damn reason, chose this moment to decide to get
chatty. "This is an appetizer."

Jarle Bjornstad snorted. "I tried going vegan," he said.
"I'd hooked up with a woman in Anchorage who wouldn't
even wear leather. It didn't work out."

"Mine's not that kind of date." Seth wondered how
much arugula, kale and flowers it would take to fill up
the man with shoulders as wide as a redwood trunk and
arms like huge steel bands. His full-sleeve tattoo boasted
a butcher's chart of a cow. Which might explain his ability to turn a beef patty into something close to nirvana.
"And there probably aren't enough vegetables on the planet
to sustain you."

During the remodeling, Seth had taken out four rows
of bricks in the wall leading to the kitchen to allow the
six-foot-seven-inch-tall cook to go back and forth without
having to duck his head to keep from hitting the doorjamb
every trip.

"On our first date, she cited all this damn research
claiming vegans lived nine years longer than meat eat-
ers." Jarle's teeth flashed in a grin in his flaming red beard.

"After a week of grazing, I decided that her statistics might be true, but that extra time would be nine horrible bacon-less years."

That said, he turned and stomped back into the kitchen.

"He's got a point," Quinn said.

"Amen to that." Having learned firsthand how treacherous and unpredictable death could be, with his current family situation on the verge of possibly exploding, Seth decided to worry about his arteries later and took another huge bite of beef-and-cheese heaven.

*Need to know what happens next?*
*Order your copy of HERONS LANDING*
*wherever you buy your books!*

## Available June 19, 2018

### #2629 A MAVERICK TO (RE)MARRY
*Montana Mavericks: The Lonelyhearts Ranch* • by Christine Rimmer
Not only were Derek Dalton and Amy Wainwright once an item, they were actually married! With Amy back in town for her friend's wedding, how long before their secret past is revealed?

### #2630 DETECTIVE BARELLI'S LEGENDARY TRIPLETS
*The Wyoming Multiples* • by Melissa Senate
Norah Ingalls went to bed a single mom of triplets—and woke up married! They might try to blame it on the spiked punch, but Detective Reed Barelli is finding it impossible to walk away from this instant family!

### #2631 HOW TO ROMANCE A RUNAWAY BRIDE
*Wilde Hearts* • by Teri Wilson
Days before she turns thirty, Allegra Clark finds herself a runaway bride! Lucky for her, she accidentally crashes a birthday party for Zander Wilde—the man who promised to marry her if neither of them was married by thirty...

### #2632 THE SOLDIER'S TWIN SURPRISE
*Rocking Chair Rodeo* • by Judy Duarte
Erica Campbell is only here to give army pilot Clay Matthews the news: she's having his babies. Two of them! But can she count on Clay—a man whose dreams of military glory have just been dashed—to be her partner in parenthood?

### #2633 THE SECRET SON'S HOMECOMING
*The Cedar River Cowboys* • by Helen Lacey
Jonah Rickard, the illegitimate son of J. D. O'Sullivan, wants nothing to do with his "other" family. Unfortunately, he's falling for Connie Bedford, who's practically part of the family, and he'll have to confront his past to claim the future he wants.

### #2634 THE CAPTAIN'S BABY BARGAIN
*American Heroes* • by Merline Lovelace
After one hot night, Captain Suzanne Hall remembers everything she craved about her sexy ex-husband. Now she's pregnant and Gabe thinks they should get married...again! Will they be able to overcome everything that tore them apart before?

---

HSECNM0618

*Days before her thirtieth birthday, Allegra Clark finds herself a runaway bride and accidentally crashing a birthday party for Zander Wilde—the man who promised to marry her if neither of them was married by thirty…*

*Read on for a sneak preview of*
*HOW TO ROMANCE A RUNAWAY BRIDE,*
*the next book in the **WILDE HEARTS** miniseries,*
*by Teri Wilson.*

*Is that what you want?* The question was still there, in his eyes. All she had to do was decide.

She took a deep breath and shook her head.

Zander leaned closer, his eyes hard on hers. Then he reached to cup her face with his free hand and drew the pad of his thumb slowly, deliberately along the swell of her bottom lip. "Tell me what you want, Allegra."

*You.* She swallowed. *I want you.*

"This," she said, reaching up on tiptoe to close the space between them and touch her lips to his.

*What are you doing? Stop.*

But it was too late to change her mind. Too late to pretend she didn't want this. Because the moment her mouth grazed Zander's, he took ownership of the kiss.

His hands slid into her hair, holding her in place, while his tongue slid brazenly along the seam of her lips until they parted, opening for him.

Then there was nothing but heat and want and the shocking reality that this was what she'd wanted all along. Zander.

Had she always felt this way? It seemed impossible. Yet beneath the newness of his mouth on hers and the crush of her breasts against the solid wall of his chest, there was something else. A feeling she couldn't quite put her finger on. A sense of belonging. Of destiny.

Home.

Allegra squeezed her eyes closed. She didn't want to imagine herself fitting into this life again. There was too much at stake. Too much to lose. But no matter how hard she railed against it, there it was, shimmering before like her a mirage.

She whimpered into Zander's mouth, and he groaned in return, gently guiding her backward until her spine was pressed against the cool marble wall. Before she could register what was happening, he gathered her wrists and pinned them above her head with a single, capable hand. And the last remaining traces of resistance melted away. She couldn't fight it anymore. Not from this position of delicious surrender. Her arms went lax, and somewhere in the back of her mind, a wall came tumbling down.

The breath rushed from her body, and a memory came into focus with perfect, crystalline clarity.

*Let's make a deal. If neither of us is married by the time we turn thirty, we'll marry each other. Agreed?*

*Agreed?*

# THE WORLD IS BETTER WITH *Romance*

Harlequin has everything from contemporary, passionate and heartwarming to suspenseful and inspirational stories.

**Whatever your mood,
we have a romance just for you!**

Connect with us to find your next great read, special offers and more.

f /HarlequinBooks

🐦 @HarlequinBooks

www.HarlequinBlog.com

www.Harlequin.com/Newsletters

HARLEQUIN®

A *Romance* FOR EVERY MOOD™

www.Harlequin.com